For
Nancy

CHALLENGE

Coffeetalk

'I tell you no lie,' said Morgan, slopping his coin-machine coffee on to the scuffed woodblock floor of the sixth-form common-room. 'Maureen Pinfold is a dream.'

Ditto stared at him in what he hoped was an enigmatic fashion. Since term began he had been perfecting this cool exterior manner, an attitude of unshakable intellectual poise.

Morgan licked dribbling coffee from the side of his plastic mug.

'She's ripe for dissection,' he said, affecting his medical style. 'I plan to operate as soon as the patient is prepared. And a theatre found, of course.' He laughed. 'It might have to be a field trip.'

'God, the mixed metaphors,' said Ditto.

'I do not believe in purity.' Morgan laughed again. He always preferred his own witticisms to anyone else's. His laughter shook another expectoration of coffee on to the abused floor. Surveying the morning-break crowd that filled the room, he said, 'You know the trouble with half this lot?'

'Tell me,' said Ditto indulgently.

'And with you too, I might add.'

'Say on.'

'They talk a lot . . .'

'So do you.'

'. . . but they've done nothing. They talk very knowledgeably about Life and Sex and Politics and Religion and all that guff. But they've got it out of books.'

He lobbed his empty mug like a shuttlecock half across the room, into the metal wastebin by the coffee machine. A group

7

standing by the bin turned and applauded. (Why did he have to be so insufferably gifted, hand and mind, Ditto wondered.)

'What's worst,' Morgan went on as if unimpressed by his skill or the applause, 'they get it out of stories. Out of lit-er-arr-tewer.'

Ditto remained studiously unmoved.

'And what's so bad about literature?'

'Literature is crap,' Morgan said. 'Fiction is, anyway. Novels and stories. It's like that coffee they make us buy. A pretence. Ersatz.'

'They ought to let us make our own,' said Ditto, draining his mug.

'You might say the same about the literature they force on us,' said Morgan and chuckled.

'Midgely says literature offers us images to think with. That its unreality has nothing to do with untruth.'

'Cods,' Morgan said. 'Images out of a book make you think like a book. And old Midge can be a pompous ass. He should have retired years ago.'

'That doesn't diminish the truth of what he's saying.'

'No, but it does make it a lot less attractive.'

'Get back to literature.'

'I'd rather get back to Maureen Pinfold.'

Ditto conceded a smile.

'You're spoiling for a fight,' he said. 'Okay. I challenge you to prove literature is crap.'

'You're on,' said Morgan, rubbing his hands with relish.

The klaxon sounded the end of break.

'Damn it,' said Ditto. 'Can't stay. Got a double period with Midge and Jane Austen.'

'Pity. I'm free. But I'll tell you what. I'll jot down my Charges Against Literature—I mean fiction—and serve them on you at lunch.'

'A subpoena I'll enjoy discharging,' Ditto said. 'But why bother? Just tell me.'

'Innocent!' Morgan said. 'My Charges will give me just the

8

excuse I need to trap Maureen Pinfold behind her typewriter in the commercial room. While she does me the favour of typing my Charges, I'll prepare the patient for dissection.'

'If this was a story,' Ditto said, 'you'd call that typecasting.'

Morgan laughed.

'Thanks for the compliment,' said Ditto, and left.

Gauntlet

CHARGES AGAINST LITERATURE

(I Mean Fiction)

Morgan v Ditto

I charge that:

1. Literature as a way of telling stories is out-moded. Done. Finished. Dead. Stories as entertainment are easier got from film and TV these days. (And what was Fiction ever about except telling entertaining stories?)

2. Literature is, by definition, a lie. Literature is a fiction. Fiction is opposite to fact. Fact is truth. I am only concerned with truth.

3. Novels, plays, poetry make life appear neat and tidy. Life is not neat and tidy. It is untidy, chaotic, always changing. Critics even complain if a story is not well plotted or

9

'logical'. (Life, logical!) They dismiss
characters for being inconsistent. (How
consistent are you, Ditto? Or me?) And they
admire 'the literary convention', by which
they mean obeying rules, as in ludo or chess.
SO:

4. Literature is a GAME, played for FUN, in
which the reader _pretends_ that he is playing at
life. But it is _not_ life. It is a pretence.
When you read a story you are pretending a lie.

THEREFORE:

5. Literature is a sham, no longer useful,
effluent, CRAP.

As I said.

Q.E.D. *Morgan*

Lunch Date

The morning over, Ditto joined Morgan in the dining hall.

An aftertaste of Jane Austen lingered in his mind as he sat
down opposite his friend. Often he went only half-heartedly to
Mr Midgely's literature class. (Morgan was right: Midge could
be unbearably pompous.) But somehow the man always riveted
his attention. Uncomfortably sometimes; he was never easy,
never made concessions and could, when marking an essay, be
ruthlessly cruel. Yet he brought to life every writer, every book
he dealt with. He seemed to devour them, making them part of
himself, and then he regurgitated them like spirits, alive, out of

his mouth, by what he said and the way he read aloud. As though he were a magician, a medium even. No doubt about it, a great talker was Midge. Had the gift of the gab, Ditto's father said—all too often these days.

While Ditto pored over the Charges and inattentively ate his lunch, Morgan prattled on. Ditto only half listened. And Morgan's voice, in any case, was almost drowned in the cacophony of three hundred people all talking too loudly as they chomped their way in concert through lumpy mashed potato, soya bean protein disguised as hamburger, and watery cabbage swimming in instant gravy.

Ditto felt sustained against Morgan's diatribe by the lingering pleasure of his morning's work. Wasn't that very pleasure itself proof that Morgan's Charges were false? Could literature really be dead, finished, if it gave him, alive, such enjoyment?

But how, he wondered, could he unsettle Morgan's entrenched prejudice? Not by argument, that was sure. Morgan was bound to win, right or wrong. How then? By demonstrating his error? Perhaps. Be scientific, pragmatic. Morgan would certainly be moved by that. *Show* Morgan he was wrong.

But how?

'You're saying nothing,' Morgan complained when the pudding was served—mushy stewed apple resurrected from dehydration and soused in the customary glutinous custard. 'Here I am, hungry for argument to distract me from the offensiveness of lunch, and you've said nothing since arriving.'

'This menu of your Charges must be digested,' Ditto replied, jabbing his spoon at Maureen's immaculately typed page. 'And your comments on each savoury item have left me no room to say anything.'

'Then ruminate privately,' said Morgan, standing up and clattering his empty dishes into a pile. 'I've a first team practice now, a full afternoon of chemistry, and I've just fixed an evening mixing it with Maureen. So the Charges found their target. See you tomorrow. So long.'

Ditto Goes Home

After school, Morgan's *Charges Against Literature* tucked into his breast pocket, Ditto sets off for home. Mode of transport: a dilapidated bicycle once used by his father to carry him to work. The sprockets squeak at every third turn of the pedals.

Ditto's legs push him on rapidly, for the weather is grey, damp, cold. But his mind is tardy. Home is not an attraction, school a livelier, friendlier place these days. The principal cause of this unhappy state of affairs—so Ditto complains—is his father.

For two years an illness has stalled the man from working. Other afflictions have resulted. A depressed and moody atmosphere in the house. Irritability. A pinching of the family's income. (Ditto's mother has had to take a part-time job behind a grocery counter to supplement their income. She will not be at home when Ditto arrives. Ditto has had his pocket-money cut, he relying on windfalls from relatives and weekend work as a window-cleaner's mate in the streets round his own to provide his private needs.)

Most unsettling of all has been the souring relations between his father and himself. They have reached that pitch where neither can speak civilly to the other for more than a minute or two; more usually, sharp words and barely controlled insults serve as their daily discourse. It pains Ditto; he is certain it pains his father. But the hurt is apparently incorrigible.

Pedalling steadily towards his next parental encounter, Ditto's thoughts travel in another direction. He remembers a time before his father's illness, before, even, he himself had left primary school.

A photograph in Mother's box of family pictures, me thin as a lamp-post on the sprout, ten years old, holding a fishing rod and grinning triumphant at the camera, a dace the size of a stunted sardine hanging from the end of my rod, the dace wriggling still when the picture was snapped by a nearby fisherman who obliged so that Dad could be in the picture too and he is there behind me and to one side, my left side I think, right as you look at the picture . . . Dressed in his work suit, grey and a bit baggy, but a starched white shirt collar and neat black tie, always neat your dad they used to say always just right, his hair still black then, grey now since his illness, and his face full still, moon round still, and used to shine blood-orange red after he'd had a few at the local in the evening or before dinner on Sundays, doesn't bother now, can't I suppose . . . After the picture was snapped he rubbed his hands together as though trying to crack the finger bones, and smiled to himself in the way he does, did, when pleased or proud, he was pleased and proud that day because I'd caught that dace my first and he had been there to see it and have the moment recorded, the capture captured, memorialized by the obliging fisherman.

That same day, yes that's right, just after slaughtering the dace with a sharp blow on its head we saw a snake swimming down the river its head above the surface like a submarine periscope. It turned just below us and writhed ashore entirely confident, not a jot of notice paid us who were standing there aghast agog me, my father, the nearby obliging fisherman, my camera still in his hands. An excited shouting boy came downriver with the snake, skipping along the bank crabwise, pointing at the riverborne reptile and bellowing Look, look, a snake, see, a snake. The minute the snake got ashore this boy and me we fell upon it hurtling stones and beating it to death in the end savagely—were we scared or were we hunting—and while we were assaulting it Dad said You shouldn't kill it. It's only a grass snake you know not poisonous . . . Afterwards he was silent did not celebrate the occasion with wringing of hands and did not join this stranger boy and myself who persuaded the obliging fisherman to take another snap of the pair of us each with a finger and thumb in tentative apprehension holding the snake by its tail end dangling dead between us as we had been big game hunters in safari Africa and our grins are wide and fevered.

If not the snake why the dace? . . . Next day I was disappointed, the snake was like a deflated balloon after a party, but a wrinkled memory of itself not exciting or fearsome any more nor wondrous neither, just empty, and pungent . . . Dad reverently wrapped it in old newspaper and carefully placed it in the rubbish bin.

And said nothing.

Home

Now, thought Ditto, he'll still say nothing. Can he still?

The front door snecked behind him, its phony pane of stained glass window trembling in the concussion. He hoped the glass would shatter one day and was experimenting with various forces of slam to find breaking point. At least when the window splintered the superfluous lead would serve at last some honest purpose and save the pieces from scattering.

Coughing from the livingroom, rich, liquid, gurgling.

A deadly liquefaction, Ditto thought. He's gargling in his own sputum.

He would have liked to climb the stairs at once to the seclusion of his room; but a sense of duty he was trying so far without success to corrupt forced him towards the livingroom. Inside, the air was greenhouse stuffy, smelt of rancid snot, stockinged feet and overheated television set. He tried not to breathe, but the only result was that finally he had to breathe more deeply still and savour the tangy odour. He sat down on the edge of the sofa, prayer-placed hands gripped between pressing knees.

'Home then,' the inevitable conversation began.

Ditto nodded, eyed his father for signs of prevailing mood, slumped there in his bulky armchair with its rubbed-to-the-skin arm ends, his feet resting on a footstool. At the other side of the fireplace the TV flicked its images but the sound was turned off. His father disliked TV sound; said it gave him palpitations, and that anyway he could imagine what was being said because nobody ever said much worth hearing.

14

'What you done today?'

Ditto resisted the impulse to reply not much. He knew too
well the fractious talk that would follow.

'Jane Austen,' he said, his throat stiff from restraint.

'What did she have to say for herself?'

Ditto squinted for hint of jest behind his father's deadpan.
None was intended, sadly.

'She's an author,' he said.

'O, aye?'

'A dead one.'

'Is she now? So you've been reading all day.'

'For exams.'

'What's she write about, this dead woman?'

'It would take too long to explain.'

A long glance; a smile, sour. 'You mean, you think I'm too
thick to understand.'

Ditto knew better than to bite on that bait.

'How've you been?' he asked.

'Fairish. Cough's bad.'

'Had some tea?'

'Couldn't be bothered.'

'Like a cup now?'

A nod; small boy ashamed. 'If you're making one.'

While the kettle boiled, he standing over it, Ditto remembered another day.

He gave me a book that time, how old was I? About twelve, well
I must have been twelve because it was my birthday and I had
just started at sec school and was getting good reports. He was
hand-wringing pleased, his lad was learning French and stuff
that would help him get on in life. A proper snot I must have
been. Am I still? . . . And he gave me this book, who was it by?
I don't even remember. Anyhow I thought it was some god-
awful person, not to be seen reading it, and I said, I remember
what I said if not who the book was written by, I said, not
thinking, you don't when you're a kid like that, I said haughty,

15

Thanks, Dad, but I can't read this. Why not? he said his face fallen. Well at school they tell us what's best to read and Mr Midgely, he said this writer wasn't very good, so I don't think I can read it you see, I said, right little snot . . . And he just looked and went out of the room, my room, my bedroom it was, I remember now, where they'd brought my presents early to please me and see me open them . . . Mother looked daggers, one of those looks she used to promise me in shops when I was very little and not behaving, If you don't behave yourself I'll give you *such a look*, she'd say, well she gave me such a look then, that day, my birthday, and went after Dad. I don't remember feeling I'd said anything rotten.

Was that the start of it?

Ditto took the cup of tea to his father.

'Ta,' his father said. 'And I forgot. There's a letter for you. On the mantelpiece. Come after you'd gone this morning.'

Ditto took it. The handwriting he knew at once; knew too that he could not read this letter here, in front of his father.

'If you're all right then I'll go upstairs and do some home-work.'

'Right-o,' his father said, an agreement heavy with accusation.

Ditto's Room

Upstairs. Front room of three-bedroom, semi-detached, late 1930s speculation-built house, half limey brick, half crumbling pebble-dash with bay-window on ground floor front room, the room below Ditto's.

Inside Ditto's room. Single bed with blue candlewick coverlet. Wardrobe, laminated dark oak on chipboard. Bookcase crammed with books, mainly paperbacks, case made by Ditto himself in woodwork lessons during first two years at secondary school, painted white and looking now to him a hamfisted construction for which, nevertheless, he felt a nostalgic affection. Old, real oak kitchen table, four feet by two, sanded to the bare

16

wood (having once been stained dark in days when virgin wood was vulgar) and sealed with varnish; now used as desk; found by Ditto languishing on a rubbish tip.

On desk: blotting pad, pocked with surreal ink stains, doodles composed mainly of abstract combinations of squares, triangles and hachured shading: product of many hours of brooding contemplation. Portable Olympia typewriter, present from parents last Christmas. Pot, unglazed, red-fired clay bought for five pence at summer fête at school, profits in aid of Oxfam, serving now as pen and pencil holder. Seventy-second scale model of Mark V Spitfire on perspex stand. Rubber pencil eraser; chipped wooden ruler; small calendar cut from last year's pocket diary and Sellotaped to a piece of stiffening cardboard.

The room walls: painted mat sand-brown, the ceiling mat white, the door and other woodwork gloss white. On the walls: pictures, clippings from magazines, posters, record sleeves, bookjackets. Ephemera in profusion. Mostly browned from age and sunlight (which achieved some sort of penetration between the hours of two-thirty and six, *post meridiem*).

The flat-faced window, two-sectioned. One section opening outwards gives view and vent on to arterial road leading to town (or, from, depending upon one's need), centre of town two miles distant, edge of town one mile. His father cannot tolerate noise of traffic, preferring duller, but larger and quieter back bedroom, hence this front room Ditto's. Window veiled by crisply starched net curtains, insisted upon by his mother (you never know what people outside might see inside). For night-time privacy, heavy chocolate-brown curtains drape the windows, floor to ceiling.

The seats. One kitchen chair, uncomfortable, at desk. One old, small, poorly stuffed armchair covered in synthetic fabric stretch-cover, bile-green, bought in Co-op sale and looking it, with bright red loose cushion for highlight. If you slouched across the thing, sitting was bearable.

17

Letter

He laid the letter on his desk blotter, stood staring at it a moment, savouring its possibilities. Its arrival was entirely unexpected; not even hoped for.

Then, anticipation weakening him so much his hands trembled, he took off his school jacket and tie, heeled his shoes from his feet, unhitched his trousers and stepped out of them, took up the letter again carefully, threw the candlewick coverlet aside, and lay down on his bed.

While calming his breath, he gazed closely at his name and address in the unmistakable handwriting: fluent, firm, yet still echoing a child's awkwardnesses.

The letter, when he slit open the envelope with his right forefinger and eased the page out, was written on one side of a single sheet of school exercise paper. As he unfolded the page, a photograph fell like an autumn leaf on to his chest, picture side down. Deliberately he left it lying there while he read the letter.

Sibena

Wednesday

Hi!

This place is a DUMP - a hole, a DEAD END. Why my crazy parents had to move here I shall never understand. There is one main street about as exciting as Noddyland, no cinema, no caff. As for BOYS - I saw one yesterday. I said

18

Hello, he said Arrr.

The scenery is quite nice.
But who wants lovely country
without a lovely boy to share it
with?

Which brings me to – You!

How art? And everyone at
the factory? Has Midge recovered
yet from the pleasure of my
leaving? And Morgan?

WRITE, please, SOON

The enclosed is to remind
you what I look like.

Hugs –
Helen xxx

Picture

Her of course, the picture is of her, of course, in colour and my
god it's her in swimsuit strip but not stripped enough, must
have been taken last summer before she left while she was still

here and I was lusting after her then and didn't attain what I dreamt of feeling too cloddish when face to face with her but she must have known   mustn't she   Morgan wouldn't have dithered the sod not he and she would have aided and abetted him I'll bet   would she me   those legs what legs what tits and a face to go with them a bit knowing though and maybe that's what held me back though it doesn't now you brute   but this letter now maybe all the time she was waiting was wanting was after it me me her after it was she me her me her legs breasts skin face legs legs o legs her her her there there there   there   there   there

and it's gone all over my frigging shirt and my hanky's in my pocket in me trousers on the frigging floor   should have thought   prepared   but didn't think   didn't expect her to send such a provocative picture the slut

But she is okay, could almost shoot off again just looking at her, certainly could in the instant flesh instead of the instant Kodak, and that's what I'd like, what I need, her in the flesh and willing.

Does Morgan succeed in all he claims?

I bet he doesn't, most of it plain rodomontade. Randy he may be but a rodomont he is too by nature. Though even if he has had only one or even two of the adventures he claims, his rodomontades are but decoration to the truth, cos then he's had it, with his willy or nilly, and I haven't.

What a thing to have to admit at seventeen years plus.

Afterbath

Ditto rose from his rumpled bed, straightened the cover, examined the scene for clues of his concupiscence, pulled on his trousers, replaced his damply soiled handkerchief in his hip pocket to dry in his fleshheat before discarding it in the laundry basket, and sat at his desk, the better to frizzle his eyes on the tormenting photograph while musing on his unexpected letter and the inexperienced nature of his being.

Suddenly, in the afterbath of his self-abuse, his room seemed tediously dull, embarrassingly naive. There he was for all to see who had gump to perceive. The inside Ditto. Himself, as he would hide himself.

The furniture was all his parents' except for the rickety bookcase, rudely cobbled product of boyhood, and his desk-table, throwaway acquisition from a rubbish dump. The pictures on the walls, like his bookcase, were stuck there three, even five years ago: expressions of crazes and passions now vestigial only: birds from his nature-spotting days (circa 11 yrs), planes from his flying period (circa 12+), authors and singers going back into primary school years, and finishing up lately with Orwell, Lawrence, Joyce and Richard Brautigan (the authors), Fineguts, Razor, Towlake and Prinwell (the singers).

Even his books were half boyhood favourites, half recent purchases mostly inspired by Midge and bought more—could it really be the truth?—because he believed they were what he should read and possess rather than simply to please himself.

And that damned Spitfire arrested there mid swoop on its transparent stand, motion miniaturized and simulated and made safe for childish hands: another pubic hangover.

All toys, the whole lot, or received possessions of other people. Where among it all was he? Where was the present Ditto, the real, bloodflushed Ditto? WHO was the present Ditto? Was this he? This neatly precise collection of outgrown junk and secondhand propositions? Loads of it crammed into this little box of a room, yet featureless somehow. Absent in its presence.

Was that what Morgan was getting at?

Remembering Morgan, he took from his jacket the *Charges Against Literature* and laid the page out, open on his blotter. By its side he placed Helen's letter and her photograph.

They lay silent there. Together.

Words on paper cheek by jowl with colours in a pattern (a reflexion of light and shadow captured months ago).

21

Mute. Yet eloquent.

Witnesses come to accuse him.

Opponents in some unlooked-for battle.

Challengers.

Perturbed in the face of his documentary friends, Ditto went to the window, pushed aside the obscuring veil, and glared out at the street.

People and vehicles programmed for home ignored him.

Ditto's Mother Returns

Hello, love.
Hi.
You all right?
Sure. You?
Tired.
Course.
Been home long?
About an hour.

Your dad seems a bit low.
O?
Did you give him his tea?
A cup. All he wanted.
Have a chat with him?
A few words.
You haven't been rowing, have you?
No, not yet anyway.

You should talk to him more.
I had something to do.
He likes a chat with you.
Yes? You wouldn't think so sometimes.
It's his illness.

School all right?
The usual.

I wish you'd spend a bit more time with him.
Ma, you know how it is.
But you could try.
I do.
You know how ill he is.
I know.
It's the illness makes him . . .
It's more than that.

Did you change your shirt this morning?
Can't remember. Think so.
Looks filthy.

Well, I'd better go down and get supper.
Anything I can do?
Lay the table, love, in a minute, eh?
Sure.
I'm worn out.
You do too much, Ma.
Somebody has to, love. But I'll manage.

Set-to at Supper

Father and I had had fights before. And frequently at meals because that was when we spent longest together. At other times, to save the conversation from turning fierce, I could leave the room, or he would feign occupation in a newspaper or the television, or, in desperation, in reading a book. But round the table at meals we were both trapped, literally facing one another, with Mother between, referee, judge, wearied peacemaker.

This evening the conversation began with the topic of my day, a sure-fire success for Father's satiric irony and my tetchiest self-defence.

23

I had, said Father with a sour chuckle, been lounging around all day talking about a dead writer. I think he intended only to be playful: to tease, not to wound. I sensed the danger, of course; my antennae were by now well trained, and Father's chuckle not exactly deceptive. Mother sensed it too, and her quick glance as she handed me my plate pleaded for neutrality.

I wished no combat; my reply was likewise intended simply as a jest returned in kind. Was apparently received so. Father smiled; Mother laughed (too gustily however; hers was not a response to my wit but an attempt to ensure the conversation was taken at its lighthearted face value).

And now we reach that significant truth which detailed description would only obscure. Despite our mutual intentions, we—Father and I—were soon spilling emotional blood. Even as I snapped pert replies to his gusty blows, I regretted—more, resented—doing so. But could not restrain myself. I did not mean what I said. I did not hate the man I said it to. I knew what I said to be clever but hurtful, witty but churlish. I knew this even as I spoke the wounding words. Nor did saying them give me any release. Unlike an explosion of temper, or an unlooked-for row, or some final show-down in which the event brings satisfaction, there was no easing of tension. Just the opposite. The longer we continued, the greater the tension became.

Father was bulged and red of face, squared to me and by the end near speechless with rage.

I felt like a twisted elastic unable to stretch any more.

Mother sat slumped, head bowed, defeated.

We reach this point every time we argue without interruption and it is this I resent more than anything, that the tension is a separating wall between us, Father imprisoned on one side and me on the other, and our only means of communication to shout insults at each other across the unyielding density. At least by that one exhausting means we each know that the other is still there.

Of all my father's assaults that evening, only one requires

record. I was, he told me, not just lazy, not just ungrateful, not just loutish and arrogant. No. I was far worse: a twit. I knew nothing except from books, had learned nothing of life from living it. I was a ponce, a parasite. Clever, I might be, but, he concluded, using a favourite phrase of disparagement, if I were faced with a real life problem, I wouldn't know whether to have a shit or a haircut.

Perhaps this evening matters went further than usual; or perhaps I reached the edge of hysteria. Whatever the explanation, I suddenly saw what seemed to me the comic stupidity of this fruitless exchange. Here were a father and son, for no explicit reason, lashing out with sharpened words at each other across a table of neglected food, spectated by a tearful wife-mother. Is that funny, comical? Not so presented. That is why I so present it. But through my eyes at the time it appeared quite bizarre.

And I laughed. Laughed as I used to do when a boy and watching some slapstick farce on television. Laughed uproariously. Side-achingly. Uncontrollably.

Father, finding not unnaturally nothing whatever to laugh at, nothing in the remotest funny, glared across the burdened table at me a moment and then collapsed, unconscious, burying his face in his untouched sausage and mash.

Morning After

'You mean,' said Morgan, 'he flaked out, right there in his mash?'

'Indubitably,' said Ditto, passing off his slopping coffee as nothing worse than yet another accident of the inadequate plastic mugs.

'Where is he now?'

'Memorial Hospital. Mother in evidence and playing at nurse —of course.'

'Christ!'

'He had not arrived when I left.'

'You are tasteless, not to say unoriginal this morning.'

'Put it down to the coffee.'

'Or the shock.'

'Let's walk the perimeter.'

The day was a wrung-out dishcloth.

We stalked the fence that bounded the school playing-field for some yards before either of us spoke again.

Then, 'Is he very ill?' asked Morgan.

'Doctor says he'll be all right in a few days,' I said. 'But that we must realize this collapse is another of the inevitable steps in the deterioration of his health and an added complication.'

'You use language like a civil servant.'

'I use the medic's words exactly.'

'Whatever could have possessed the man?'

'A desire to avoid the words *disease* and *death*, I suppose. They aren't fashionable. Besides, nowadays doctors are civil servants.'

We had reached the sports shed where are stocked grass cutters (various) and equipment (assorted) used by the plodding groundsman. Against the south-facing wall of the shed (which happened also to be the wall hidden from view of the school buildings) was set a wooden bench upon which the groundsman himself usually lazed. Today he was not there.

Morgan and I sat.

'Do you want to talk about it any more?' asked Morgan.

Ditto glanced at his friend stretched at his side, back to shed, hands buried deep in trouser pockets, legs stuck straight out in front, feet crossed, and had a sudden intuition that explained something of Morgan's success with others. Girls especially. He was unafraid to ask questions, to touch on raw nerves, but to ask and touch gently. It was a quality Ditto had not recognized in Morgan before and admired the more for wishing he possessed it himself while knowing he did not.

Morgan caught his glance and smiled.

'There is little to say,' said Ditto, turning his gaze on to the backs of the houses whose gardens ran along the other side of the wire-mesh perimeter fence. Were they being spied, he wondered, as others had been before, by one of the unoccupied occupants who would report to the Headmaster by telephone that two of his pupils were lurking behind the sports shed and why weren't they engaged more fruitfully in scholastic activity. 'I do know though that home is claustrophobic.'

'The suffocating womb.'

'Maybe.'

'There's an answer to that.'

Ditto took from his inside pocket a twice-folded page from a school exercise book. 'Which brings me to the business of your *Charges Against Literature*.'

'By what unlikely route?'

'I'll tell you,' said Ditto.

Ditto's Progress from Collapse of Father to Moment of Previous Conversation

Course of Events: Collapse of father. Summoning of ambulance. Father, accompanied by Mother and Ditto, rushed to hospital, where treated for heart attack. Ditto and Mother remain until Father reported 'out of danger', when, at 10.30 p.m., persuaded to return home. Mother sits up all night, unable to lie down or to sleep. Ditto goes to bed, sleeps fitfully, but wakes finally at 4.45 a.m. and cannot sleep again. So gets dressed, has tea with Mother, then sits in own room coping with Emotional State (see below). During this time sees possibilities explained in *Some Truths about Ditto*, para 6, below. Writes *Replies to Charges*. Has breakfast, 8 a.m. Leaves for school. Sits through first two lessons distractedly. Meets Morgan for coffee during break.

Emotional State: From supper at 6.30 the previous evening till conversation with Morgan, suffers succession of assaults:

SHOCK at father's sudden collapse;

27

PANIC while waiting for ambulance;

HORROR at sight of emergency treatment—efficient, fast, crypto-violent—leaving no doubt that father in danger or of prospect of father's imminent death;

GUILT at his part in bringing on the attack;

SORROW for same;

RESIGNATION: What could he do now? What would be would be, etc;

DESIRE to amend;

RESOLUTION to effect amendment;

RELIEF when told by telephone that father likely to recover, even if in no better state (and, so implied, perhaps even worse state) than before;

NEED to talk to someone about it all: thus conversation with Morgan.

Physical Effects: Intense activity, followed by trembling debility, succeeded by aching coldness. Sleep, fitful. Early waking, feeling washed out, listless, discordant, nervy. Remained thus throughout morning, with aching tiredness slowly drowning the discordance till afternoon when body felt hot inside, cold out, and filleted.

Intellectual Effects: Mind at first unable to cope. A tumble-drier of pictorial images passing chaotically before inner eye. Psychedelic derangement. But after early waking, begins to re-assert some semblance of control. During this period, physically cold and uncomfortable, begins to see connections in clear-minded strobe, which become by breakfast a coherent rationale. In other words, understood matters before obscure to him. As if the events of the night have somehow 'blown off' meaning in his head. This understanding he composes into *Some Truths About Ditto* and *Document: Replies to Morgan's Charges*, in order to focus and record his thoughts, and give his hand some dis-placement activity, thus diverting himself from the horrors of the memory of the last twelve hours.

Some Truths About Ditto

In the past few hours a number of things have become clear to me. Reaching this understanding has been painful. It is not comfortable being honest with oneself. I have no intention of reliving the painful self-examination, nor of plodging about in a self-pitiful discussion about the things I have come to realize. Instead I shall simply enumerate the Truths.

1. I find myself both loving and hating my father. This appals me and I wish to do something about it. Yet I know that to-night's catastrophe is likely to be repeated—with even more terrible results—because neither of us can cross the barrier of our self-created antagonisms. We cannot, to be plain, talk to each other openly and honestly. And we both fear to show the love we have for each other. Why, I do not know. But struggling to know has decided me about:

2. I must somehow get away from home, for a few days at least. The distance is necessary to help me sort out where I am. More: what I am. I feel this as a bird, perhaps, feels the need to migrate. A compulsion. Do it, or die. It is as though home were making me impotent.

3. Which brings me to Helen. I know now, looking back, that the frustrations bred by her letter, my randy desire unsatisfied, spawned the irritation which spoke at supper and consummated Dad's anger. I want to have it off with Helen, I know. But do I fear the act? If not, why have I not? Starkly, the truth: yes. A truth not easily told.

4. And here around me as I scribble this laundry list of emotional dirty linen are the symbols of my rag-bag being. Last year's toys, other people's gimcrack. What is mine? Me? My own? I feel like a caterpillar chrysalised and about ready to slough off the carapace, that imprisoning lumber from a former life. I will not be so contained. I will not hide among the detritus of other people's beings, or settle for childhood's pleasures. I want more than that. And now I know I must work my muscles to get free.

5. But I have been too cautious. Perhaps that is why I feel so constrained now, when Morgan (so it seems to me) does not. I have not experienced enough for myself. I must set about looking for new moments. Must widen my repertoire of living.

6. So I have devised a plan: Next week is half term, seven days in convenient gift. I shall go camping. That will get me away from home, give me the distance I need to begin sorting out myself and my father. And I shall look for experience, welcoming what comes—pure sensation if that is all that's going—for action, event, drama. I shall test my caution a little. And the main event shall be:

7. The sexy Helen. I shall invite her to go camping (ho ho) too, meet her half way, at mid-point, pointing at her mid, no doubt too, for an encounter with but one goal, one eye to bull. In short —though at pleasant length, I hope—I shall lay her, the first that ever shall be.

And all this shall be raw material to my other purpose: an answer to Morgan's misminded Charges.

Document

Reply to Morgan's Charges
It is crap that literature (I know:
you mean fiction) is crap. I could
Easily reply to you in kind. But that
is not the best answer. It would only
be an argument. And you, Morgan,
being an activist, a doer - as there
ought, by your own confession, to be
many able to bear witness - prefer to
be shown, a demonstration.

So shall it be: I shall
demonstrate.

I intend a jaunt. What I have not
recorded there, however, is that I
also intend recording the events of
my jaunt, as they happen (or shortly
thereafter). And this record shall
be xx my fiction, the raw material for
it anyway.

But to counter your charges, my
fiction shall obey certain rules:
1. It shall not be written in the
manner of our logical stories. It
shall take what form it cares for at
any moment - which means whatever form
I feel like giving it at the time of
wx writing. I do this because you
feel fiction is contrived, designed
to fit certain pre-set ends. I shall
use whatever styles of prose - or
verse, or writing of any kind - I
wish to use and which seems best for
what I want to say.
2. I shall record as honestly as I can
what it is I experience and wish to set
down. And I shall set something down

however insignificant it may seem at the time, and with or without connections with anything that has gone before.

3. We shall see then(to take your charges on):

    a) whether the story of my jaunt is entertaining or not;

    b) whether my experiences are lies, though they are certainly a fiction -- aren't they?

    c) whether the ends are tied up or not, and whether their logicality is so weakening;

    d) whether this game is a game at all, or a pretence; or not. Whether it is unlike your and my life or not.

Maybe I'll surprise you.
Maybe I'll surprise myself.
Maybe it will all be quite unexpectedly unexpected.
Who knows?
But before I begin there is a question to be answered:

Who is Ditto?

Ditto is
  Thin, wiry, given to being lanky.

Brown-haired, undistinguishedly cut, worn long over the ears, fringy and thickish.

Green-eyed, tending to short-sightedness. (He ought to have visited an optician by now but loathes medical treatment of any kind, dental most of all, and is vain about the owlish effect given him by glasses.)

Slim nose, wide mouth, lips tending to thickness, above a chin that is square and juts too much for his liking.

Complexion pale. (You look a bit peaky healthy adults usually tell him.)

Right-handed. When interested in something requiring manual skill is reasonably able; when uninterested becomes manipulatively incompetent, a state of affairs he calls being psychologically spastic.

Dresses to the left—as he looks at things.

Has thin legs he prefers to conceal in trousers, rarely venturing into the machismo of showy beach clothes.

Feet, size 9 narrow.

Height, five feet eight inches (work the metric out for yourself, genius).

Total income per week: £3.00 pocket money from mother (which makes him feel guilty under the present circumstances but which he rarely refuses); £4.00 on average from work as window-cleaner's mate, an earned income dependent on the weather and the mood of his employer as well as on the fickleness of his will to get out of bed each Saturday morning early, as:

Hates getting up in mornings and likes staying up late at nights.

Temper uneven. When discouraged tends to sulkiness. When on a high, tends to impulsive loquacity.

Generally, and when on best behaviour, much liked by mothering older women. Among contemporaries, liked by a small group of those who know him well and by everyone else, as are most people, entirely ignored. Feels no need to belong to what he calls 'mobs of people'.

So far, if you are none the wiser you are a great deal better

informed and may add in the space provided any other attributes
you think important and which you note or deduce from a study
of these pages, previous and to come:

....

....

....

Of course, we must not forget:

A virgin. Though, as we have seen, a virgin not without
urgent desire to change his state, nor without surrogate practice
in preparation for that transition when it comes, if you'll pardon
the pun.

Three Conversations

I

Hello.
Hello?
That Helen?
Yes . . . Who's this?
Dee.
Dee?
Yes. Dee.
O! Dee! Well, hello!
I got your letter.
I'm glad.
Got your . . . picture.
Like it?
Certainement. Très jolie.
I didn't do it.
Eh?
French. Didn't do it. Not clever enough.
O, ah . . . but beautiful.
But not clever?
Did I say that?
By omission.
Hey, listen . . .

Can you do anything else with the telephone?
There have been attempts.
Communications pervert.
I wanted to ask you.
That's not possible on the phone either.
You're a telephonic hussy.
Spoken like a true rapist.
Listen, Helen, I've got a plan. This next week is half term for us. You too?
Yes.
Well, I'm going camping . . .
Really! Darling, you should have told me. I'd have understood.
Stop foolin', will ya. I've got only one more tenpence left. I wondered if you'd like to come along. Or rather, meet me half way?
Do you ever talk in anything but double whatsits?
Only when people don't think in them.
Parry. I think, though, I catch your . . . shall we say, meaning?
Ach, zo. And?
Love to.
Great. Here's the plan . . .

2

Hello, love.
Hi.
You all right?
Sure. You?
Tired.
Course.
Been home long?
Half-an-hour I suppose.
Telephoned about your dad yet?
Not since this morning.
I rang at one o'clock.
How was he?

35

*About the same, they said. Comfortable as could be expected.
Whatever that means. Poor man.*
Don't cry, Ma. He'll come through.
You coming with me to the hospital tonight?
Course.
Good lad. He'll want to see you.

Next week is half term.
You'll be home then.
Well . . . I thought, if you can manage . . . I thought I might
go camping.
O?
Well, it's something for school as a matter of fact. A project,
sort of.

Dad won't be out of hospital for a few days yet. Not till I get
back anyway. I'll be back before they let him home, I mean.
I see. Probably.
Would you mind?
You won't be far from home, will you? Just in case.
Same place as I went with Morgan last year. I can phone the
hospital every day. And if you . . . I could get home easily.

Your dad'll miss you.
He'll be all right, Ma. He'll be well looked after. But what
about you?
Me? O, I'll be all right. I can manage. Someone has to.

I always have.

*You go camping, love. The break will do you good. Do you good
to have a change and some fresh air for a few days.*

I'll help you with the supper. Then we'll go and see him.
Ta, love.

36

Hello, Dad.
Hello, son.
Did I wake you?
No, dozing, that's all. Nowt else to do here all day.
Good to see you.
Aye?
Sorry I couldn't come in with Mother. They only let us in one at a time. Ration us, you see!
Aye. Anyway, makes it like two visits, 'stead of one.

Feeling better?
Not so bad.
They look after you?
Fine. Fine. Not like home, you know. But they do very well.
What about the other patients? Do any of them talk to you?
Haven't felt much like talking yet.

Dad, I'm sorry about the . . . the other night, you know.
Aye? Me too.

Not much sense in crying over spilt milk, is there?
Suppose not.

Looking after your mother all right?
She doesn't take much looking after, Dad, you know that. I just get under her feet, really.
All the same, me in here, you're the man in the house. She'll need all the company she can get.
She manages very well, Dad. Really. In fact, if I was out of the way as well she'd get a bit of peace and quiet for a change.
It can't be easy for her, me in here.
It's a rest for her.
She must worry. You know how she is.
It's a break from her usual grind, Dad. Change is as good as a rest.

She always did worry too much, your mother. A wonder she's not in here 'stead of me.

I brought you some grapes. Least, Mum bought them. I carried them.
Thanks.
When she left you just now she had to go off to the social security about something or other.
Couldn't you have gone for her?
They said it had to be her.
Bloody bureaucracy.

Dad, I have to go away for a day or two.
Go away? What for?
I have to. Sort of school work, you see.
School work?
A project. Only a day or two.
Couldn't you explain? About me in here. Your mother on her own.
Mam will be fine. It won't be for long. And it's the last chance before A levels.
Your exams? Can't go wrong with them. But she'll be on her own.
I'll phone twice a day. See she's all right. And that you're okay.
Doesn't matter about me. It's your mother I'm thinking of. On her own, in that empty house, worrying.
She'll be perfectly all right, Dad, and I'll be back before she's felt the miss of me.
I don't like it.
I'm sorry, Dad, but I have to go.

Are you doing all right at school?
Smashing, Dad. Very well.
Working hard?
I think so.

How's that dead woman?
Jane Austen?
Aye, her. All right, is she?
Fit as a fiddle!
Better off dead than alive, then, isn't she.
Wouldn't say that.
No, maybe not.

I'll have to be off, Dad.
Aye, right-o, son.
Good to see you.
Thanks for coming in.
Take care.
I'll try.
And mind them nurses.
Can hardly raise me arm never mind owt else.
See you, Dad.
So long. And here . . .
What?
*Mind you get back from yon jaunt as soon as you can. You don't
fool me, you know.*

Tarra then.
Aye.

JOURNEY OUT

View from the "27"

If this were an old-fashioned story—the kind you, Morgan, so anathematize—this could be the beginning. The foregoing would be excoriated by the inventor's pen and omitted finally, or be revamped as flashback, that worn device of the suspense mongers. But this is not one of those old-fashioned stories, is it? Though it is, for me, a kind of beginning. Journeys always are, aren't they?

The bridge out of town, across the river, allowing passage from County Durham to Yorkshire, humps beneath us, a pleasant undulation, providing glimpse over its grey stone parapet of ling-brown Tees, in swirls, urgent, full-bedded, passing beneath.

The Tees is diarrhoeic today: a consequence of spring rains elutriating Pennine bogs and peat. I digress, Morgan, only to entertain your anti-dithyrambic turn of mind.

Why is it I wish Morgan were here now?

To return to the matter in hand. The tantalizing vision not just of a willing but of a lusting Helen. And of a harassed mother and a stricken-prone father. The pursuit of the one inflames in me guilty feelings at my desertion of the others. But without feeling there is no guilt. So my guilty feelings provide proof of my filial affections for those from whom I seek escape.

Ha.

Maybe that is what this journey is really all about? Ineluctable evolution. Proving myself to myself, if to no one else. The strivings of my independent spirit.

Getoutthereladandshowthemyoucanstandonyourowntwofeet.

Ffossip.

'She should have had more sense,' said the ageing driver-conductor to a rotund passenger of the female gender standing by the open bay of the driver's cab in flagrant disregard of the bus company's rule published in a notice posted above her head.

DO NOT STAND ON PLATFORM
WHILE BUS IN MOTION

'Well,' said the passenger, 'there's many a slip.'

'Aye,' said the driver, 'nor but it's happened before.'

'And happen it'll happen again,' said the passenger.

'What 'tis to be young,' said the driver.

'Nay,' said the passenger, 'nowt like it, is there!'

They laughed; knowing.

LIMBSOME... LITHESOME... LOVESOME said a neon-glowing advertising panel above a window.

Picture accompanying words: a pair of dismembered legs of the female gender, arranged like pretty boomerangs, dressed in tan-coloured tights.

Intention of advertisement: to sell women's stocking tights by suggesting that they will transform every wearer's legs into limbs of the sort pictured. Mine too?

Ha.

He took from his wallet, where he had carefully placed it, Helen's previously provocative picture, and smiled. She needed no tights.

There was that time when I was about eight when we still lived in the country at One Row, seven or eight anyway, before you really know what it's all about, Mickey and me were wandering back home down the path through the wood when we saw a

41

gang of older kids ten of them maybe all about ten or eleven as well and all of them crowding round looking at something in the middle of them and they were grinning and nudging and excited but keeping it quiet because, you could tell, they didn't want to attract the attention of grownups who might be nearby but they didn't pay Mickey and me any bother and we went up to them and edged our way to the centre and they had a girl there who wasn't much older than eight herself maybe nine and they'd made her lift her skirt and drop her pants and show them herself . . . None of them touched her they just looked as they would at a new kind of toy in a shop window everybody taking a turn in front of the girl to bend down and look closely so that the crowd was circling slowly and bending and rising like a slow circling wave or an endless queue of courtiers processing round a queen and bowing to her . . . We had a look Mickey and me then went off back into the wood again and sat on a log side by side not saying anything at all just shivering, trembling, giggling at each other . . . When we recovered we wandered down the path home and the crowd had gone and the girl had gone and we had not seen the girl's face because her skirt had been held up in front of her all the time we were there. And when we got back to our street there was Mickey's mother and mine standing outside our back gate in their aprons with their arms akimbo watching us come and muttering to each other frosty faced so we knew we were in trouble. We know where you two have been Mickey's mother said when we got up to them. You nasty little beasts. You get home my lad and don't you dare do anything like that again. But my mother just looked at me not speaking till after she had given me my tea when she looked at me again for a minute before she said You know they could have crippled that poor girl for life . . . I puzzled over that for days afterwards but couldn't understand how she could have been crippled just from us looking at her but no one said . . . When Dad was told he just grinned at me when Mother wasn't looking. And winked.

Ditto beat a retreat from his memory, replacing Helen's photo-

42

graph in his pocketed wallet. Richmond was in view.

On Richmond hill there lived a lass
More bright than May day morn

Ho ho

RICHMOND, Yorks. Pop. 46,500. Ec Wed. Md Sat.
Situated on hill-top dominated by 11th Cent. castle,
now ruined, built c1075, commanding superb view
across R. Swale. Walls 11th Cent. but most surviving
military structure 12th Cent. Castle originally entered
from town through gate-tower, converted late 12th
Cent. into base for 100ft high stone keep, still standing.
At S.W. corner remains of original hall containing
domestic quarters. Legend claims Robin Hood held
captive in Robin Hood Tower in N.E. wall; also that
King Arthur's Knights lie sleeping beneath the castle,
waiting for the time when a brave man awakens them
to save the world from disaster.

Town built round one of the largest and finest
market squares in Britain, continental European in
feeling. Narrow alleyways lead off, locally called
'Wynds'. Also: Georgian theatre, in use, dating from
1788. Green Howards' Regimental Museum in crypt of
Holy Trinity Church standing in centre of market
square, unique example of church with shops beneath.
Baden-Powell, founder of Boy Scouts, once lived in
tower in S.W. corner of castle.

Apart from historical and legendary associations,
this attractive little town possesses considerable
architectural beauty and great scenic beauty. Visit
recommended.

Bus Stop

Ditto descended into the market square. The bus journey had
been an experience. Insignificant, commonplace, undramatic
perhaps, but an experience: his reason for journeying.

And what was the nature of this experience, this bus journey?
He contemplated the question quarter-mindedly as, hitching his
pack on to his shoulders, arranging straps and frame comfortably, he plodded off, boots cobblestone-ringing, into Walter

Willson's, there to buy a can of McEwan's Export pale ale, before making for the castle, where he proposed finding a sunny, sheltered corner which offered a view up the river. There he could sit and enjoy his meal.

Nature of bus experience*: consoling, comforting, contenting. Vehicle warm. Motion tranquillizing. Moving view—seen from his snug seat—of passingly pretty interest despite having seen it many times before. The whole provocative of piquant thoughts and sensational images. Unhurried, unworried. Cocooned irresponsibility.

Is that why so many people like travelling?

Maybe, he supposed, his mind turning to thought of his mother's always perfectly made (just moistly right) tomato and egg sandwiches and wedge of apple pie. And the McEwan's, for which his thirsting tastebuds goosepimpled. One thing about a bus trip, it coated your mouth with dehydrated diesel oil.

He sought out his favourite spot in the castle, where the south-west wall breaks from Scolland's Hall into a tumbling defile, a rift in the defences that slips dizzily to the road and river a hundred feet and maybe more below. There is a ledge wide enough to sit on and stick out your feet, where you are hidden

---

*All right, all right, I admit it! I got this idea for telling my tale from *At Swim-Two-Birds* by Flann O'Brien (which I have been reading recently with, I might add, often puzzled pleasure). But then, to be fair, I expect he pinched it from somebody else. (Nothing is safe these days.) But from whom? James Joyce I'll bet. I've discovered that almost all the interesting things contemporary writers do they get from his *Ulysses*. Which I have never managed to read beyond page 27. (I've only tried twice, I confess. But Midge says everybody talks about *Ulysses* and how it is the greatest novel of the twentieth century but that few people have actually ever read it right through to the end. So I don't feel *that* guilty. I've a few years left to try it again.) But working on the principle that there is nothing new in this world, where did Joyce get the idea from? I asked Midge. He said, 'Good question. Probably from Duns Scotus, or one of those forgotten Jesuit theologians Joyce was brought up knowing about at his ghastly school. It sounds to me like the kind of way Jesuits would argue. But go and find out for yourself, lad. Why expect me to know and do all your work?' Typical Midge!

from treading tourists unless they brave the edge. There today the sun shone uncooled by a breeze, and from there the broad sweep of the river and its vee-shaped valley can be seen stretching away up the dale. So there he sat, bum cushioned on folloped groundsheet, back pillowed by pack placed against Scolland's ruined stones.

Sandwiches, pie and beer he set safely firm on the ground, in reach of his right hand.

Quiet.

But a quiet made of surging Swale, fast, full from rain in the hills; a lark ascended, singing; wind soughing in trees furring valley sides, new green blinking in the breeze, sun-flashed. Blue sky. White flock clouds islanded. Grey stone.

An active peace.

Suntillating

No sooner had I enjoyed my small repast and had settled myself to a sunbathed repose than I was discovered by a youth perhaps a year or maybe two older than myself.

Description of intruder: Tall, well-built, mongrel-handsome. Dressed in regulation jeans, dungaree shirt washed to faded pale blue, open to fourth button, revealing hairless tanned chest, muscled. Hair brown, thick, long, tending to curls, casually (but carefully) arranged. Eyes blue, alert; nose narrow, straight; mouth thick-lipped, wide, smiling. Teeth white, sound, attractively irregular. Donkey jacket slung over shoulder perhaps a touch too self-consciously nonchalant. No other portables.

'Watcher,' he said, sitting himself crosslegged at my in-castle side with athletic, look-no-hands smoothness.

Nature of remark: Friendly, inviting conversation, in Geordie (i.e. Tyneside) accent.

For an irritated moment, I resented this disruption of my cosy, somnolent pleasure. But I reminded myself of my resolve, of the very purpose of my adventure. Here was an opportunity of precisely the kind I wanted, an opportunity for new experience, for something to happen, and it was being offered to me unlooked for.

I shifted my slumping torso into a more welcomingly attentive, upsitting posture.

'Watcher,' I replied, assuming as nearly as I could my new companion's tone and inflexion, as a deliberate means of ingratiation.

'You haven't seen my mate, have you?' he said. His eyes were searching me out.

'Who's your mate?' I asked.

'You don't know my mate?' he said, surprised. 'I thowt everybody knew my mate.'

'I'm not from Richmond,' I said, apologetic.

He regarded my cushioning backpack. 'No, 'course. Sorry,' he said without sorrow.

(I remarked to myself again how not knowing what people without reason expect you to know at once lowers your stature in their eyes. Lowers their interest in you anyway.)

'Mind you,' I said, unable to prevent myself attempting further ingratiation, 'I can't see much from here and there's been nobody in sight while I've been here. And I've been here about half an hour.'

'He's not been then,' said my companion. 'Just like him. "Meet me in the Castle about twelve," he says when I saw him this morning. "We'll go for a drink." We never go into the Castle for a drink so naturally I come here. But he'll be there already, propping up the bar. Impatient swine.'

He laughed.

Nature of laugh: Indulgent chortle, not irritated.

Comment seemed inappropriate; I smiled to show willing.

'I don't know why I bother with him,' he went on. 'Take last night for instance. Meet him half-seven at the billiards, he tells me. "We'll have a bit of a game and a bit of a giggle with the lads," he says. I get there at quarter to eight—I knew he wouldn't be there before then no matter what—and I wait around like a spare part till nine. Then he strolls in, grinning like a ninny, and

46

I can see straightaway that the smile is all show. Really he's got a right beat on, so I don't say owt to upset him, and he just picks up a cue and knocks hell out of the balls for twenty minutes before he says a word. And then he doesn't say much more than "Buy us a pint, kiddo." I could have thumped him.'

He repeated his former laugh.

This time a remark seemed necessary to maintain the conversation.

'Then why didn't you?' I asked, affecting genuine interest.

'I have before now, I can tell you,' he said, giving me a glance.

Nature of glance: Collusive, implying that this confession was just between ourselves and that I would understand what others might not.

'I had a go at him just a few nights back. He'd messed me about all day. We ended up in a pub in Catterick. I was in a right mood by then and he started playing up. Having a go at me, you know, in front of a gang of soldier boys that were boozing in there. He gets ower big for his boots at times like that, shows off a bit. So he's giving me some stick, taking the piss like. Well, I've had enough like, and a pint or two, and all of a sudden me stomach hits me eyes and I grabs him and waltzes him out the back into the car park and gives him a right leathering. He's smaller and thinner than me so he didn't stand much chance with me losing me rag, you know, I'm pretty bloody when I'm in a paddy, but by god he still managed to bend me nose about and make me pant. He's game all right. I think he wanted a fight, mind, and he knew I'd not damage him too bad, us being mates, you know, so he went prodding on till I lost me blob. He knew I would. He knows my limits, like. Same as I know his. And if you can't have a good scrap with your best mate who can you have one with? You know what I mean, I expect.'

Morgan.

'Yes, I know,' I said.

'It's a grand day for the race,' he said.

'Which race?' I said.

'The human race,' he said, and laughed.

'It is,' I said, smiling through his mockery. 'So why didn't you thump him last night?'

'Wouldn't have been right.'

'Why not?'

'Well, he has this father, you know. Anywhere for a big apple he is, a right crawler. They don't get on. Always rowing. And I could tell they'd had a set-to last night before he came to the billiards. So I laid off. But I was still fed-up with him all the same.'

'Why didn't you go and join him in the pub then, if you know that's where he'll be?'

'No fear! Last night was last night. This morning's different. You can't be giving in all the time. He can stew in there. After a bit he'll feel guilty and come looking, all apologetic and smarmy and trying to make out it's all my fault. "Why, Jacky," he'll say, surprise surprise. "What you doing here? I thought we said we'd meet in the pub, man. I've been waiting half an hour, till I got worried about you and thought I'd better look for you out here. I'm sorry, mate." Like that, you know. But he doesn't fool me.'

'You known him long?'

'About six months. He picked me up one day when I was hitching from Scotch Corner toward Brough. I was making for Liverpool, as a matter of fact. But he brought me here and we hit it off that well we started knocking about together. I stayed on here, got a job labouring for a builder doing some work round Easby Abbey, down the river, you know.'

'You got digs to stay in or what?'

'No, no. I've got a room at my mate's house.'

He seemed surprised I had not understood his domestic arrangements without asking. At which my courage failed me to inquire further. Nor could I have done. For at that moment a shadow fell across us. There standing in the eye of the sun on the wall behind us was a youth who could be no other than Jacky's mate.

Description of Jacky's mate: Please enter below your preferences for Jacky's mate's appearance and features. Note well: he must, of course, be handsome (in your eyes if in no one else's) and he must for the sake of this narrative be about eighteen. Jacky has also said that his mate is shorter than he; but then Jacky is over six feet tall and heavyish, so there is plenty of room left for your own imagination and predilections:

Proposal

'I'm sorry, mate. I've been waiting for half an hour, till I got worried about you and thought I'd better look you out. I thought we said we'd meet in the pub, man? What are you doing hiding here?'

'What did I tell you?' said Jacky to me but squinting up at his mate, his eyes dazzled by the haloing sun.

'Like that, is it?' said Jacky's mate, smiling.

Nature of smile: Acidly competitive, inviting tart rejoinder.

He jumped down from the wall and sat on the sloping bank facing us, his hands bracing his body upright. A puff of wind, it seemed, might send him scudding down into the valley deep at our feet, like a child skidding down a helter-skelter.

'This is my mate Robby,' said Jack to me, but still looking at his friend. 'The one I was telling you about.'

'Been telling you about me, has he?' said Robby, glancing at each of us in turn like a cat eyeing two neatly cornered mice.

'The purr you hear,' said Jack, looking at me this time, 'is not Robby's laugh. He has a laugh like a ball of wool.'

'What fun! A new friend!' said Robby with monotone sarcasm.

'You had a bad night,' said Jack.

'And a worse morning,' said Robby. 'But entertain me. Tell me about your—cough cough—friend. What's his name? Introduce me, social moron.'

There was at this point within me an irresistible rise of gall with the attendant side-effect of spontaneous anger. At such moments I have no courage nor any restraint. I merely react. Is that what wins V.C.s? Unthinking, unwishing, I said:

'Why don't you get stuffed.'

There was between my two companions that satisfyingly shocked hiatus which succeeds such unexpected outbursts from an apparently mild-tempered and disadvantaged stranger.

Then Robby rolled on to his side, beat upon the turf with an excited fist, giggled with unnecessary exaggeration, and gasped:

'Great! Marvellous! Terrific! Isn't he beautiful! Hasn't he just drummed us, Jacky!'

While this demonstration was in stagey progress, Jack, grinning but not smiling, leaned towards me and muttered:

'Go steady, kiddo.'

'I'm going nowhere,' I said in matching reply, 'till I'm ready.'

'Here, I say, you two,' said Robby, pushing himself up and climbing across us into the eye of the sun again. 'Let's go to the pub. We'll have a pint. I'll treat you. How about it, drummer boy? You game?'

'If your mate is,' I said.

'Sure he is, aren't you, Jacky? Nobody ever heard Jacky Thompson turn down a free pint.'

Jack stood up, as smoothly as he had sat down, Arab-fashion, and sómehow unexpectedly graceful given his size and solidity.

'Aye,' he said, 'come on, kiddo.'

Pubtalk

'Politics,' said Robby when the pints were ringing a table in the corner of the Bishop Blaize, 'now there's a subject to keep off in a pub. Sex and religion being the other two.'

'Nowt much else to talk about,' said Jack, raising his glass.

'Sport maybe, if you like that sort of thing. But you're not going to start on all that again, are you?'

'I've a question to put to our new friend.'

'Look out, kiddo. Trouble.'

'Kiddo can look after himself all right,' said Robby. 'So much is known.'

Jack sucked at his beer. 'A nice drop that Camerons,' he said. 'Good enough to curl your toenails.'

'I take it you're on the right side,' said Robby, ignoring Jack. 'Roughly anyway.'

'Is there ever a right side?' I said. 'Rough or otherwise.'

'An intellectual!' said Robby and honked a laugh that drew staring glances from other parts of the room.

'Listen who's talking,' said Jack. 'Karl Marx resurrected.' He stood, drained his glass, belched. 'My round,' he said and went, casual, to the bar.

'No more for me,' I called to his back.

He flapped a dismissive hand.

'Of course there's right sides and wrong sides,' said Robby in an indivisible tone.

Indivisible: Because earnest, unwilling to banter, arrogantly assuming authority.

But then, I thought, he's been like that all the time, despite appearances to the contrary. There's a manic note in his emotional coloratura. A result of his running battles with his father? And does like always attract like so surely as this? If so, then Jacky is in the deep end with his father too! Must find out.

'You can't opt out of commitment,' Robby was saying. 'Either you're for or against. There are no fences left to sit on. Not any more.'

'Only slogans to rant?'

'You have terminal apathy and gangrenous cynicism.'

'Don't mistake healthy scepticism for pusillanimous indifference.'

'Nor your epigrams for truth.'

'I wish they had Newcastle Exhibition here,' said Jacky returning triple-glass-handed. 'Right nectar that stuff is.'

He sat down, shaking slopped beer from his hand.

'Unlike this beer,' said Robby, sipping delicately from his brimming pint, 'kiddo here is all head.'

'O, aye?' said Jack, 'a bit frothy, is he? And how should he be?'

'You know the trouble with intellectuals?' asked Robby.

'You tell me, clever lad,' said Jack.

'They are so busy sorting out all sides of the argument they never get round to doing anything.'

Jack raised his glass to me in salutation, winked, lifted his eyebrows, and sank his pint in one unbreathing swallow.

'Consider Jack the dripper,' said Robby. 'He doesn't think too much, but he knows where he stands. Knows what it's all about. Don't you?'

'If you say so,' said Jack putting down his glass. He belched again without restraint, wiped his mouth with the flat of his hand and said, 'I could go a nice pork pie, I know that. How about you?'

'See what I mean?' said Robby. He tossed a fifty pence piece among the beer glasses and swill. 'Here, I'll stand you.'

'Not for me, thanks,' I said. 'I had something in the castle.'

'Not our Jack, I hope,' said Robby.

'Lay off, eh?' said Jack, and went off to the bar again.

'How did you meet him?' I asked.

Robby eyed me in sharp, askance amusement for a moment.

'He got fed-up of home,' he said, 'and decided to have a breather for a while. See some places, you know. His dad gives him hell. Always nagging at him . . .'

Bingo.

'. . . Used to thump him about till Jack got too big and might thump him back. His mother tried to interfere once and he gave her a going over as well. Very pretty. You'd think Jack would be the aggressive sort after all that, but he isn't. As placid as flat beer, aren't you, Thompson?'

Jack returned with two cylinders of pork pie clasped in one

hand and a brimming pint in the other. 'Talking about me behind my back, are you?' he said, sitting.

'He's telling me about your father,' I said. 'Fathers interest
me.'

'Nowt much to tell. He's all right really, the old sod.'

'See?' said Robby to me. 'He's not just placid, he knows
where he stands. His father brings him up by hand and our hero,
here, leaves home to taste the delights of travel. Ah, you might
think, a classic case of filial rejection. But you'd be wrong. Our
hero has every intention of returning, actually and metaphoric-
ally, to the familial hearth, there to resume his hard-won place.
As soon as he's bored with the pleasures of the wide world,
home he'll scarper and take up life where it left him off. He's
just having a holiday, aren't you, Jacky lad? All this is just
excursion. Knows his roots, does our Jacky, and he'll be happy
enough to go back to the ground where he was planted.'

'You could be right about that,' said Jack, his pint once again
raised to help on its way the pie he had consumed in two bites.
'Do you want yours?'

Robby pushed his pie towards his friend. 'No, take it. Your
need is greater than mine. We can't have you losing your figure.'

'Ha ha,' said Jack, and consumed the second inadequate
refection.

Robby drained his glass, placed it on the table and stared at
me with that kind of brass-faced grin that means 'your turn'.

'You'd like another?' I said.

'Thanks, kiddo,' said Jack.

When I sat down again, wet-handed, Robby and Jack were
finishing a muttered conversation all too obviously about myself.

'On a hike?' asked Robby nodding at my pack lying by my
stool.

'A few days.'

'On your own?' asked Jack.

'Till tomorrow.'

Robbie: 'Meeting someone?'

'A friend.'

53

Jack's scatological laugh.

Robby: 'A girl, eh?'

'Once aboard the lugger and the girl is mine,' Jack sang, the beer fomenting a tune and an uninhibited performance. 'I'll bet you're a bit of a horizontal champion in your quiet way, bonny lad.' He guffawed and wagged a prim finger. 'Be careful, kiddo, or you'll dip your wick once too often.' He reprised his bawdy outburst.

'Looks like you missed out,' said Robby to Jack.

'O, aye?' said Jack, draining his glass. 'That depends on what I wanted in the first place, doesn't it, Sunshine?'

'Idiot,' said Robby and laughed.

Neither laugh nor conversation included me.

'All right now then are we?' said Jack.

'Champion, man,' said Robby, mock-Jack. 'Much relieved. And it's time you were making tracks.'

Jack looked at his wrist watch. 'It is an' all. Are you going to have a word with kiddo here?'

'I'll see to that. You get to work.'

'See you.'

'So long.'

Jack said to me as he stood up, 'Maybe we'll get together later on. So I'll just say tarra. Thanks for the pint.'

I had suspected for the past few minutes that I was becoming inane. Suspicion now was confirmed. To Jack's goodbye I could do no better than smirk and wave a collapsing hand. It was at that very second I realized the cause of my disintegration: the same as my urging desire to visit the lavatory. With some surprise I heard my voice speaking my ponderous thoughts to Jack's retreating figure: 'I've had five pints.'

Jack turned at the door. 'Down but not out,' he said and was gone.

'He's a nice bloke,' I was saying to Robby. 'I like him.'

'I'm glad,' said Robby, tolerant as a barmaid. 'I think he likes you too.'

His tone was sobering.

'You're extracting,' I said, but with careful effort.

'Never!' said Robby. 'But listen. What are you doing tonight?'

'Dunno.'

'I've got something to do this afternoon.'

'I think I'll have a sleep.'

'But tonight, after six, Jack and me have an amusement planned. Would you like to join in?'

'What you going to do?'

'Come and find out. Don't want to spoil things by telling. It'll be a surprise. How about it? You game?'

'It'll all be experience, won't it?' I said.

'It will for sure,' said Robby smiling.

'Where'll I meet you?'

'Let's say here at six-thirty. Okay?'

'Okay, but listen, I've nothing else to wear but what I've got on.'

'You'll do just fine. Just beautiful.'

'I really have to go out the back.'

'Enjoy a good splash. I'll see you tonight.'

'Half-six. Here.'

'You've got it. And one thing I will tell you. I bet afterwards you'll really know where you stand.'

'Nigmatic.'

'And irresistible!'

Robby went through the street door. I went through the door labelled

Graffiti

FAR AWAY IS NEAR AT HAND IN IMAGES OF ELSEWHERE

Ponderoso

Beer has made me tired plus getting up early and being in open
air so much   not used to all that   I'll have a kip in
the sun in the castle just where I was before just here
out of the way   nice   out of the wind too   but
can see up the valley   nice   pretty   ah

Don't know what to make of them two, those two, are they?
Dunno. Interesting. What do they do? if?

Skylark. Pretty view. Thought that before. But still true. Skylark. All that energy, larking about in the sky, all that work,
flying like demented, like in love.   Ah. Sex more like.
Larking in the sexy sky.

I can't even sing, never mind fly. What hope for me with sex?

England: lark, liquid, above a hill, verdant, blue sky dazzled
with pillows of clouds. Wordsworth and Vaughan Williams,
though I prefer Benji-the-jazzman Britten myself, who is
English enough too thank the lord.

And what's this they're up to tonight? Getting brave aren't I,
accepting such uncertain invitations from complete strangers.
What would Morgan say! Ah, Morgan, thou shouldst be with
us at this hour. Crap. He'd say I was a timid sod. Mayhap he'd
be right. How do you get like that? The prisoner is of a nervous
disposition, m'lud, and when attacked by five armed warders
cowed in a corner of his cell in a cow hardly way. Man's a fool.
Yes, m'lud. I sentence you to eternal anxiety and don't let me
hear from you again. Or is it learned? Mother always worrying.
Was she worrying when I was born? Was she at that mystic
moment wondering whether Dad had remembered to leave a
message for the milkman? Two pints today, please, we have an
extra mouth to feed. Was she, even, Shandy-like, unnerved by

some mundane distraction at the climactic moment of my con-
ception? Or maybe Dad's right: that I know nowt except from
books, am a pseud. Wonder how the old bloke is, poor chap.
Always loathed being ill. Incapable. Like a hobbled animal.
Raging against the indignity, the frustration, the loss of control.
Rage, rage against the dying of the light, old man. With nowhere
else to live except in his body what else do you expect? But that's
an insult. To say he can't think. He can think. But he thinks by
feeling and knows what he thinks by seeing what he does. Me,
I know what I think by seeing what I say, like the poet said. Is
that the difference, the real difference between us? Is that why
I can't understand him and he can't understand me? Not the
generation gap—crap that is—but the education gap? The
thinking gap. Is that why he can't explain him to me and I can't
explain me to him? He wants me to show him what I am, I
suppose. Wants to see I'm like him by acting like him. Is that it?
God knows. And He isn't too chatty. Is that why I'm here now
doing all this? To try and show him? To try and convince myself I am more than he says? Could be all he wants, if *I* want?
And are Robby and Jack what he wants? Jack reminds me of
him a bit, as he was before his illness, as he must have been,
judging from photographs, at my age. Good boozer, hard
worker, one of the lads, a bit of a joker, good looking. A handsome feller, they say my dad was when he was young. They say
that about Jack, I don't doubt. But there he is having a hard
time with his dad, so what's his dad want of him? And Jack says
Robby is always rowing with his father. Though in his case it
sounds like he wants his father to be something different from
what he is instead of t'other way about. A flipping father trio.
Morgan doesn't have

Salutation

'A penny for them.'

Helen. In full flesh bloom. Better than the photograph. I
could hardly look at her but in snatched glances. Shyness is an
illness and ought to be medically treated.

57

'Hey! What . . .?'

'Meeting you, chump.'

'But I thought . . .'

'To get here I had to tangle a web. Officially, by which I mean parentally speaking, I'm here on a three-day state visit to my father's brother, otherwise known as my uncle, and his family who live in Gunnerside. I told you I'd find a way.'

'Very convincing.'

'In one hour I embark on United's three-o service going forward to Reeth, where I shall be picked up by father's brother's wife, a child-weary mother of eight, one more being imminent, a prolific breeding record I regard as more suitable to rabbits than human beings. On arrival and after a suitable time has passed, I shall casually mention to my bucolic uncle that I met by chance here in Richmond, as indeed I have, an old friend, verily a school pal from my Darlington years, who invited me to a social evening (ahem ahem) . . . well, go on, invite me . . .'

'O, of course, please join me for an ahem social evening tomorrow.'

'Thank you kindly, kind sir. Tomorrow it shall be. And, I shall continue, I would appreciate it if they would allow me to accept and keep the appointment. They, of course, only too glad to be spared an evening of my stay without my adolescent presence, will say yes, but be careful. And I shall meet you where'er you will. Okay?'

'Do you really have to strain the truth so brazenly?'

'Did you?'

'Touché.'

'Maybe I should go out and come in again?'

'Sorry.'

He had had a picture in his mind of how this meeting would go and it was not like this. She talking so much, he tongue tied. He hated being taken by surprise, unprepared. Surprises always turned him sulky. He did not know why but called it shyness.

Helen knelt at his side, bent down, and kissed him. A gentle caress; unmistakably inviting.

58

'I haven't come sixty miles for a discussion about morality,' she said. 'And you've been boozing. I can smell it. And taste it now.'

'Further apologies. I met a couple of blokes and had to keep my end up in the pub.'

'Masculine crap. And that wasn't exactly the end I thought you'd come here to keep up.'

'Thank you for your confidence in my abilities.'

They laughed at last.

'Why is it always so difficult to be natural when you're meeting someone again after a long gap?' she said, settling herself at his side.

'Any prizes for the answer?' he said, shifting on to his side so that he could keep her reclining figure in view.

'You never know your luck.'

'Try fear.'

'Silly! I'm not scared of you.'

'O, yes, you are. Just as I'm scared of you.'

'How?'

'In case you've changed. Not what I remembered. Or expected.'

'And?'

'Better than.'

'Thanks, kind sir.'

Castle-gazing tourists ambled by, pretending the two recumbent figures they had surprised themselves by discovering were not there. They looked pointedly at the view.

'Are you over your fear yet?' she asked, her eyes closed to the sun.

'I'm recovering fast.'

'Good.'

'Are you okay here or do you want to go somewhere else?'

'The sun is warm, we're out of the wind and nearly out of sight. The grass is soft enough. Why move?'

'There are people about.'

'My, what a private soul you've got.'

59

She sat up, supporting her body with her arms, her head hanging back full-face to the sun. Beautiful. Provocative. Unknowing? or coy design?

'No,' she said. 'I really do have to get to my uncle's. Mother knows my e.t.a. and will telephone to be sure I've arrived.'

'I know the feeling.'

'Cloy cloy.'

She sat cross-legged; plucked at the turf between her knees. 'Why must they?'

'Yours always seemed pretty easy-going to me.'

'A front. In public they affect a liberal nonchalance.'

'At home?'

'They have three different locks on each of the outside doors, burglar-proof catches on all the windows, and they keep a chromium-plated fire extinguisher under their bed.'

'The latter necessary to douse the ardour of your father's passions.'

'Which explains, no doubt, why the extinguisher has never been used.'

They laughed.

'So they're running scared,' he said.

'For them life is an obstacle course littered with booby traps.'

'And their little girl is always in danger.'

'That's how it used to be. I was ten before they stopped worrying about baby-snatchers.'

'And now they worry that you'll get raped.'

'Wrong. They could almost cope with that. I'd be the injured party, you see. All their expectations about life would be confirmed and they'd have me at home to nurse and coddle all day.'

'So what's the problem?'

'They think I'll do the raping. They don't say so in as many words, naturally. That's the infuriating thing. They pretend to be concerned, and warn me about men who are after only one thing, as they put it. But they can't hide what they are really thinking, that I'll go out and lay any man who takes my fancy.'

'And get yourself pregnant.'

60

'No, no. You still don't understand. That's just what a man would think.'

'So I'm a man!'

'And cute with it. I'm sorry. It's just that I'm all stewed up about them at the moment.'

'Join the club.'

'There was a row, you see, about my coming away.'

'So what should I know that men never do? Tell me, I'm truly interested.'

'Sure? I don't want to bore you. We both came here for some fun, remember.'

'Which is just what you're telling me your parents are worried about, isn't it?'

'You're getting warm, I'll give you that!'

'Fun and games. Hanky-panky. And actually I'm boiling with frustrated passion.'

'I should have brought the aforesaid extinguisher. Actually, they use phrases like that: hanky-panky and fun-and-games. Would you believe? You see, if I got preggers that would confirm their beliefs about life. Another of the traps. And if I liked the bloke and married him that would make it all right. I'd be properly trapped, paying for my mistakes, taking the consequences of my actions—all that guff. And I'd be there, lumbered, for them to cluck over still, giving advice, and, what's best, with a baby for them to feel sentimental about.'

'And all forgiven.'

'Of course.'

'But if you had fun, played hanky-panky and didn't get with child?'

'I'd be a loose woman. I'd be promiscuous and, worst of all, I'd be enjoying it. I'd be an unpaid whore, a happy hooker, a woman of easy virtue. Etcetera. That's what bothers them most.'

'Ugly words.'

'Ugly sentiments.'

'But never said straight out?'

'O, no. That's what makes it so horrible. I don't think I'd

mind if they came straight out and said what they think. Trouble is, I suspect they don't even know that they think it. So it all comes out in innuendo, by implication. And somehow, that makes everything worse. Dirties everything.'

Ditto thought of his father; their rows; their straight words. And of his mother, with whom he rarely discussed or argued about anything. (He had promised to telephone home this evening and must not forget; he owed them that, and was glad to discover he wanted to keep his promise.)

'The other way can be as bad sometimes, you know,' he said. 'People say wounding things in anger. And words said can't be unsaid.'

'I'd take my chances.' She stood up. 'My bus leaves in a few minutes.'

He stood up too and leaned back against the wall. He felt an impulsive desire to probe her presence with him now, to hear her reason it. He knew before he spoke that his question was a mistimed curiosity. But could not help himself.

'Just tell me one thing before you go.'

She looked at him, her face still betraying the feelings their conversation had revived. But he could not hold back.

'Why did you send that letter and your photograph?'

'Ask no questions and you'll get no lies,' she said. 'But if it bothers you—'

She turned and all but ran from the castle.

'Helen!' he called.

But she did not stop; and he did not follow.

He pressed his back against the wall. Hard. Bruising stone on brittle bone. Till it hurt. Sharp, clean pain.

His eyes guarded the castle gate against her return. (She *must* return.) While his mind picked himself to pieces.

Fool. Idiot. Clod. There is about you an instinct to disruption. I have noticed it before, often. I could list a number of such occasions but it would be tiresome. Cloth-head. Why don't you just shut up sometimes. You like to get something going nicely and then upset it. You have few talents but your skill in this is consummate. Like a small child building sandcastles and then smashing them down because the sea might get them. You pole-axed or something. What chance again. Stupy. Why. To stop anything coming too close. Is that it. Afraid to be known. To be vulnerable. It's so. Admit. Foolarse. Afraid what you'll learn about yourself. True. It is. Pity 'tis. Twit.

Unthought conclusions sent him sprinting from the castle, be-longings left abandoned by the wall.

In the market place he stopped. The Reeth bus was there by the cross, its engine running.

He reached it, panting, searched the windows in panicky haste for Helen's face. He found her in the middle of the farther side, sitting on the inner seat, a solid farmwife between her and the window. She was staring straight ahead, her face impassive, but tears coursing her cheeks. He knew she knew he was there, agitated in the road. He reached up and placed both hands flat against the window. 'Helen!' he called and slapped the glass with his hands. The farmwife turned a fierce, embarrassed face to him. 'Helen!' he called again. But she would not look. The bus door closed, the engine revved, pumping exhaust about his feet. He scrabbled in his anorak pocket, found a ballpoint pen, the slip of paper they had given him at Walter Willson's check-out. The bus's brakes blew off; he heard, as he scribbled, the gear engage. Licked the slip of paper across his writing, slapped it on to the window just as the bus accelerated away.

He had scrawled one word.

Interlude

I've had enough for a while. Am in need of light relief. Anyway, there is now a passage of time between Helen's departure and my next encounter. I did nothing after she left but mope about the place, mentally and emotionally flagellating myself. I have no intention of going through all that again here. It is so embarrassing. So please take it that this space covers the intervening three hours. Use your own imagination to fill in the details. Why do I have to do all the work!

Telephone Call

Hello?

Hi, Mum, it's me.

Hello, love.

How is he?

Not so hot, love. How are you?

I'm fine. Is he worse?

I don't know. They don't tell you anything.

They must say something, Ma.

O, they say don't worry and he's as well as can be expected. But what does that mean to anybody?

Should I try and telephone him?

I shouldn't, dear.

Why not?

It would only upset him.

Why? How could it upset him? I'd have thought he'd be pleased to hear me.

He'd be pleased to see you.

But he can't, can he? He can talk to me though.

That's just it, dear. Your dad thinks you should have stayed at home with me, you know. It would upset him to talk to you on the phone. And that would only make him worse.

He might get another attack.

Another attack would kill him.

Do you want me to come home now?
I'll manage, it's all right.
But do you want me to come home?
You're there now, love, you might as well do what you went to do.
I'll come if you want.
Ring in the morning. He's low but he's not on the danger list. He'll be all right.

Goodnight, love.

Goodnight, Ma.

Downer

Six-fifteen: Ditto is in the public bar of the Bishop Blaize. By six-thirty he has downed two pints of best bitter and is staring at his half-consumed third. Never in his life has he consumed so much alcohol so quickly. A sharp-pained headache is brewing across the left side of his skull. With fierce concentration he tries to deal with a confusion of conflicting emotions.

He feels guilty at leaving his father and mother for a less than necessary purpose. He is annoyed at himself for feeling guilty, an annoyance compounded by anger at allowing guilt to oppress him. Helen's rupturing departure adds anxiety to this recipe for depression; and frustration. If she maintains her disaffection, his journey is wasted and his desertion of home and parents a squandered ordeal.

Of course, this self-scourging is accompanied by a chorus of conditional justifications. *If* his father had not been so provocative, he would never have suffered his heart attack in the first place. But, Ditto knew, whatever the cause of the trouble, a break would have happened between them sometime anyway. After all, he had to gain his independence somehow. Etc., etc.

65

The concatenation is universally scripted from an early age; why torture us all by rehearsing it again here?

What disturbs Ditto most of all as he glowers at his beer through inexperienced boozer's wet eyes, is an undercurrent to his storming emotions, the meaning of which he cannot yet be certain about. In that calm centre where our sanity takes refuge at such times, he wonders if it is fear that his father will die while he, Ditto, is nefariously absent from the family hearth that gives him greatest distress? Or is it something less reprehensible?

(In his present self-abnegatory mood, he will not acknowledge himself able to feel anything honest and noble. But between mental brackets he toys for a moment with the prospect that this gripping undercurrent, the real engine of his turbulent feelings, is a grieving love for the man who lies now drugged to unconsciousness in a starched hospital bed attached to bottled life by plastic tubes. But the thought is unbearable and he slams closing brackets across the words.)

At which moment, six-fifty-three precisely, enter in high-stepping temper the awaited pals.

'Kiddo has turned to drink,' says Jacky.

'So we can down him,' says Robby. 'I'm glad you smirk, drummer boy, and glad to find you raring at the ready for our evening's adventure.'

'We'll just have a pint or two before we go,' says Jack.

'If we must,' says Robby. 'Though kiddo looks as if he's had enough already.'

'Get stuffed,' says Ditto, sour from his thoughts and his beer.

'I just have,' says Robby, 'and even I need time to revitalize my vitals, as it were.'

He sits at Ditto's side, patting his arm, which Ditto draws away.

'Fear not,' says Robby, 'there is no danger.'

They wait, silent, till Jack has placed three pints on the table and sat down facing them.

'Our friend,' says Robby to Jack, 'is on a downer. I recognize the symptoms. And know the remedy.'

66

'A good stiff drink is what he needs,' says Jack.

'No, no. Adrenalin. That's what he needs. The smack we manufacture for ourselves without aid from doctors and other pill pushers.'

'Stop nattering and sup your beer,' says Jack.

'One last word, executioner. I'll lay you both a bet—nay, will lay you both if you like—our adventure tonight will revive kiddo's flagging spirits a treat. You still game?'

The question is unavoidable.

'Maybe,' says Ditto, not without difficulty. 'Depends what you want to do.'

'Don't toy with your glass then,' says Robby, 'and look at me when I'm speaking to you.'

Ditto cannot help an involuntary glance and an unwilling smile.

'Ah, so it's the old gags you like best! We have vays of making you vile,' says Robby, his laughter infectious. 'As for this evening, dear friends: we begin with a public meeting, after which —doubt it not—you will be only too happy to engage in the titillatious romp I have in mind, a mystery escapade, an assault upon the bastion of boredom, an attack on high-toned hypocrisy, an antic night of convention breaking.'

'You're a right windbag when you try,' says Jack, drains his glass and stands. 'Come on then, Sunshine, one more before the fray, then we'll be off.'

Party: Political

Seven twenty-six. The market hall. Stale with aftertaste of festering vegetables. A cavernous hangar with concrete floor, windows high under iron-strutted roof-without-ceiling. An assortment of stackable chairs laid out in melancholy rows. A gaggle of forty-or-so people scattered about, leaving the first two rows and six ranks at the back yawningly empty. Down one wall, three trestle tables, scarred and bruised from their more usual market duties, bearing cups on saucers, plates of plain biscuits, bottles of milk, bowls of sugar, and a tea urn, all attended by a balloon-bosomed daleslady in blue print dress. At the front, another trestle table, this time its market-worn skeleton shrouded in a motheaten green velvet covering. Two chairs behind. Pinned, botchily, to the front of the covering a poster, wrinkled with crumple-creases: GET GOING WITH LABOUR.

Enter the three escapaders.

'I hope you are going to behave yourself tonight, young man,' says a voice from behind. A cockerel of a fellow peers at Robby, a knotty, tweed-jacketed, open-neck shirted man with a toothbrush moustache. A man with a mission, a belligerent in the Great Battle.

'Why, comrade,' says Robby in mocking astonishment, 'we can assure you categorically that at this time we have no intention of disruptin' the deliberations, though I must take this opportunity to warn you that we reserve our constitutional right to engage in legitimate dissent if we feel it necessary and any attempt to prevent us exercisin' our democratic rights will effect consequences for which we cannot be 'eld responsible.'

'Look, laddie,' says the man, 'don't get cheeky with me. I don't give a damn who your father is, if you start messing about, out you'll go—along with your poncey pals.'

He pushes our three friends aside and parades down the aisle to a seat in the first occupied row, where with nods and thumbjabbings and animated mutterings, head turnings and hitchings of his body-bulging jacket, he indicates to his companions the presence of (and, no doubt, his recent exchange with) Robby, who, during this pantomime, seats himself in the empty back row, Jacky on his one side, Ditto on the other.

As soon as I sat down I knew I was not normal. Since leaving the pub I had felt like an arthritic marionette. Stiff but unable to stand unaided. My headache, during the two-minute walk supported on either side by my companions from the pub to the market hall, had gone from volcanic eruption to flushing sodasyphon. In my inside, I wanted to be sick; on my outside, I was uncannily aware, my face wore a popeyed grin. I did not know where I was being taken, nor by now did I care.

'Why are you fetching me to the dungeons?' I said as we entered the hall, for so it seemed.

An exchange took place between Robby and a cantankerous custodian. I listened and understood their conversation entirely.

'We must behave ourselves and damn our fathers or he will mess us about,' I said earnestly to Robby when we were seated and I had recovered from not having to stand up.

'That's about it, kiddo,' he said and patted my knee.

I considered the room carefully.

'Why are we attending a prayer meeting?' I asked.

But received no reply.

'Or is everybody sleeping?'

'Dreaming,' said Robby. 'Wakers asleep. No more.'

'Someone should tell them,' I said.

'I doubt if they'd listen.'

'He's never that tight on five pints,' said Jack.

'Who?' I asked, leaning across Robby to hear Jack's reply.

'Never mind, Sunshine,' he said. 'We'll look after you.'

Robby pushed me back up straight in my chair.

Two men appeared at the table in front of the serried rows. One sat. The other stood. The seated one disturbed me. I felt I knew him. The face: features of it instantly recognizable, other parts unknown. A disturbing visual cacophony.

'Comrades,' the standing man said in a gravel voice. Tall, balding, mush-faced, prunesqualler. 'Our guest this evening needs no introduction. We all know of his many achievements and of his commitment to the working class struggle.'

I watched and listened and sawheard in minddazzle.

Went on the standingman, 'government people solidarity people people party people policy party left people party-strugglesocialistwelcome'

A waterfall of fryingpan exploding lightbulbs.

The standingman sat, the sittingman stood.

And spoke; an eloquent precision.

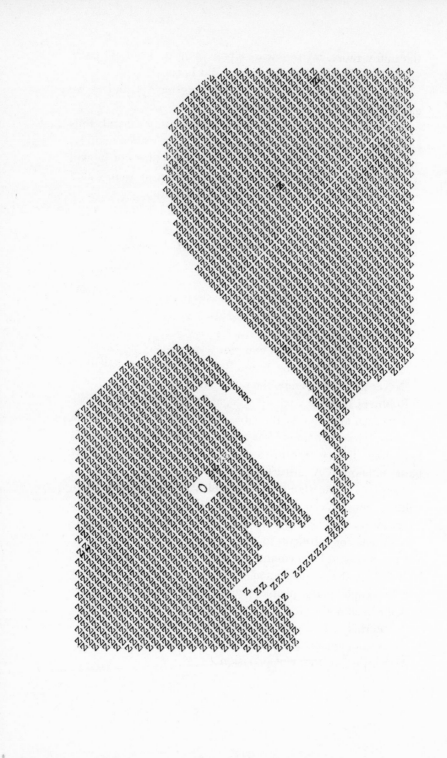

The sittingstanding talking man sat.

Fryingpan exploding lightbulbs waterfalled again.

'That was a load of elephant's,' yelled Jack through the cascade.

'All balloon,' said grin-grimacing Ditto.

Robby was Vesuvius before Pompeii got its historic come-uppance.

The hall silence. The standingsittingman stood again.

'stimulating honest peoplecomrade grateful socialist questions'

The again standing standingsittingman sat again.

Robby suddenly was standing at Ditto's sittingside, leaning forward, hands white-knuckled grasping the green tubular steel frame of the infront canvas-covered chair.

'I would like to ask our speaker when, if ever, he intends to demonstrate his solidarity with the working class by putting his considerable income where his not inconsiderable mouth is?'

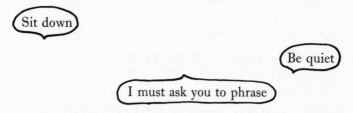

'Furthermore, does our speaker condemn absolutely the hypocrisy of those who live by preaching the doctrine of socialist change, let's not use the dirty word revolution,'

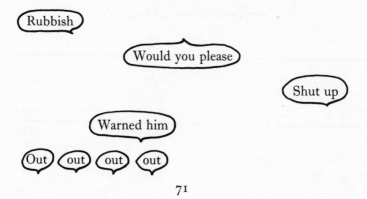

71

'while they themselves hold shares and directorships in important capitalist firms,'

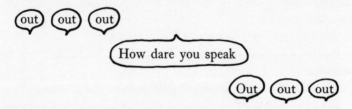

'not to mention their willingness to compromise on such matters
as nationalization, the public schools, the maintenance of the
House of Lords,'

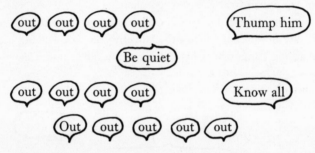

'and the careful use of backhanders, sinecure jobs, personal gifts
and spurious business deals to sweeten local party officials'

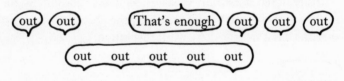

outrage	*thought Ditto*	shout out
outspoken	*rising*	lash out
outlandish	*to his*	lout
outmoded	*feet*	get out
outsider	*like*	fall out
outside	*a skinned diver*	move out
outback	*surfacing*	flout
outwit	*from the depths*	shout
outcast	*of an echoing*	cry out
outright	*pool*	right out
outstay	*into the*	stay out
outpour	*drumming torrent*	pour out
out	*of a thrashing waterfall*	out

'When will you sleepers wake!' yelled Robby as the surge engulfed him.

Ditto panned for Jacky; could not find him.

'Don't potter, Thompson,' he yelled, ablaze and hurling himself at the trembling surge breaking over Robby.

Chairs atomized.

A table subsided beneath assaulting bodies, spraying coruscating china in smithereens.

Trip in regain dodge balance fling forward to rescue and combat support, did Ditto.

An advancing bonewall.

Party: Paean

When he woke to consciousness, he wondered if it was really him lying there.

Sound of water.

Sound of trees.

Sound of breeze in trees.

Sound of water.

Feel of stone.

Hard feel of hard stone.

Feel of breeze, cool.

Smell of green.

Smell of brown.

Smell of breeze over water.

Smell of sick.

Beer-vomit.

He retched. Jack-knifed up, sitting, doubled, turned, threw up. Was clinging to an edge of stone and heaving into a flow of water inches from his obeisant face.

'Back in the land of the living at last, kiddo,' said Robby. 'We thought for a while we had lost you for good.'

The spasm remitted. He swilled a hand in the refreshing river. Performed with his palm a reviving baptism. Carefully lifted himself from the brink and took his bearings.

Late evening; a sunglow in the low sky, enough to pick out warmly the familiar lines of Easby Abbey poking from the trees above a bend in the river, upstream. There was opaque squint and sparkle on the wrinkling backwater pool at his feet, further out a grassy little knot of an island all but reached by humping boulders, the river curling into frothy little rapids between. On the bank, across, trees cushioned upwards, a fringe to the bellying field uprising beyond to the arching blue sky sweeping dome above the cave of trees under which he and Robby and Jack were.

Robby and Jack stretched out in luxurious ease on either side of where he must have lain, each with open cans of beer in their hands, their evening-paled faces regarding him with amusement.

'That was better out than in,' said Robby. 'Sit down before you fall down.'

'I'm okay, I feel better.'

'Have a swallow,' said Jack, holding out to him his beer can. He sat between them.

'Seeing I've just unloaded the last lot, I doubt I should.'

'Hair of the mongrel,' Jack said. 'Make you feel on top again.' He took the proffered can.

'How did I get here?' he asked.

'Brought you in my car, then carried you the few yards down here to this Elysian waterhole,' said Robby.

'I must have been knocked out.'

'Either by the thug who rammed his fist into your face or by the floor you fell upon. No one bothered much with the finer details.'

He drank a tentative mouthful of the beer. Surprised: he enjoyed both taste and swallow. Then, reminded of the blow to his chin, he prodded and gently manipulated his jaw. No damage, but a sore bruise.

'I have to tell you,' said Robby, chuckling, 'that that was not the only time you spewed this evening.'

'O, god, not in your car?'

'Nothing so ungracious.'

'Where then?'

'Shall I tell him?' Robby said to Jack.

'You will anyway,' said Jack.

'You must understand,' said Robby, snuggling his back into the bankside, 'that after you were so rudely despatched, the fracas came to a sudden stop. Which is just as well, considering you were prone in the path of the stampede. Our venerable chairperson—you remember him?'

'Vaguely. The standingsitting man.'

'Eh?'

'Never mind. Go on.'

'Well, he steps forward, our brave captain, folds you masterfully over his shoulder—he's learned all the fireman's lifts, has our Hector—and marches down the hall. Just as he reaches the door you decide—or rather, your stomach decides . . .' Robby tries to restrain the laughter welling in him, '. . . decides . . . it has had enough of Hector's . . . of Hector's . . . Hector's shoulder stuck in it . . . and you . . .'

'O, no!'

'O, yes . . . threw up. All down his back.'

Ditto too is laughing now. 'Like a waterfall,' he gasps out.

'Just like!'

'Out, out, out!'

'Right out and down the back of Hector's best blue Sunday suit!'

'O, glory!'

'You're a daft pair,' says Jack, but he is holding his sides too.

'It was great,' says Robby. 'I've never seen a crowd lose interest in anybody so fast. Our Hector dumped you like a bag of garbage on the pavement, and disappeared double quick into the bog. I was hustled out after you by my friends and neighbours. The doors were slammed behind our backs, and presto! All was over!'

'No more than you wanted, I'll bet,' said Jack, recovered and able to drink his beer again.

'Could never have hoped for such a magnificent finale, bonny lad. Pure delight.'

Laughing so much made Ditto feel ill again. Vaguely, not specifically. The river at their feet swirlgurgled, sounding cool and clean and of melancholy purity.

'I feel filthy,' he said unexpectedly.

'And sound solemn,' said Robby. 'We can't have that. What you need is a good bath. That would work wonders. We've no bath, but we have plenty of water. Take a swim.'

'Leave him alone,' said Jack. 'You always have to be messing folk about.'

'I'll settle with you later, deserter,' said Robby, and stood, grabbed Ditto's feet, heaved on them, swinging him at the same

79

time so that he was lying along the edge of the river bank.

'No, gerroff,' he shouted, clawing at the ground to save himself from the water.

But Robby was laughing again; giggling rather.

'Strip him!' Robby yelled at Jack.

Jack did not move. 'Do your own dirty work.'

'No no!' Ditto shouted.

'Yes yes!' Robby replied, lunging for Ditto's trouser belt.

'Off! Off!' screamed Ditto, grabbing Robby's clawing hands and with desperate effort trying to turn himself and his assailant away from the water and his trousers.

Jack sprang to his feet to save himself from the rolling, struggling pair.

'Grab him, Jack,' Robby called.

Jack climbed higher up the bank and sat on a mossy boulder, vantage for the fray.

Suddenly it was essential to Ditto that he be free. No longer a game. His frivolous dissipate energy at once focused bleakly to that end. Firmly, he took grip of Robby's wrists, twisted body and arms, pulled, lunged, leaped, hurled himself in clean rhythm.

Robby was carried, surfing, upon the wave of Ditto's determined bore. Clasped together like lovers they rose from the scuffled ground.

'Submit, fool!' Robby cried.

Each pushed the other away; but each held to the other.

Their push-pull upset the poised balance of Ditto's determined rise.

They hit the water like felled trees with snared branches, at the same instant.

Robby rose from the shallow depths first, like a jack from its box.

'Victory!' he crowed, and danced a plodgy jig in the churning pool.

Firemuse

They made a fire of flotsam and dead branches, stood by it, sat by it, lay by it, and dried. Jack did not help, but sat on and on on his boulder, drinking his way through a six-pack of Newcastle Brown, saying nothing.

Night came, starry, still. The wetness steamed from their clinging clothes in the glowheat of the fire. Activity left them now happier to be cosy and unmoving, with nothing to say, each more comfortably comforted by his secret thoughts.

Ditto was remembering another fire, another chilly night, hardly more than two years ago before his father's illness prevented them living a normal life.

Together he and his father had been fishing up the Tees on some private water. They had lashed the river all the warm sun day but with little luck. Nothing to show, in fact, but one or two middling-sized dace, nothing special, no trout which they would most like to have landed and had hoped to catch when they had set off that morning almost at dawn in a sharp clean sun, the country washed by rain overnight, the air frostdew bright. A glisten. A sparkle. A kind of carnival in birdsong silence. A good day all day, a companionable day. They had not talked much, a few words now and then about bait or pools promising to cast upon. Nothing dissentient. They did not row then; that came later. Over lunch—coffee from a flask, mother's meat pie, cake, an apple each—they had twitted one another and joked, his father in good form, anecdotal, as he always was at his best and when happiest, but not frenetic as he could be when he had had a drink or two in the evening. Relaxed. Ditto had liked him then, loved him, felt proud in a way he could not explain to himself or to anyone else. But he knew now, thinking, that it was the man's simple delight in his day of freedom from work, in the beauty about him, his absorption to the point of obsession with his fishing: these were the things which gave him his self and were attractive and made Ditto proud. And Ditto knew at once then, that evening as they sat by their makeshift fire his father and he, that he was not as this man. Knew that he fished to please him by pretending absorption, not living it as his father did. He had spent the day like this to please his father not because it gave himself the kind of pleasure his father took from it. And did that matter? He did not know, could not decide, knew only that finally he did not want to do anything simply to please this man his father. Wanted to please him of course, but not to please him by pretence. He wished to do what was of himself, his own-him. And he wondered if his father knew this.

Whether his father did or not, from that day Ditto found he could not quite, ever, please his father again. No matter how much he tried, no matter how he acted out the pretence or how fervently he wished to recapture the closeness of that day, the last day of so many that had gone before, he could not. It was as if knowing he had pretended made it impossible ever to pretend again, whether he wanted to or not. His father always seemed to sense the lie. And it was from that time that the arguments, the disagreements, the fractured days began.

From that time, too, his father's illness took hold. Was that coincidence? Or consequence?

He did not know that either. And groaned aloud in the firelight, as people do when they want to push guilt and fear from their thoughts.

'Sounds like you're ready for some more excitement,' said Robby, rousing from his own reverie.

Fireplan

Soon after midnight Robby proposed that we now set out on the second part of his plan for the evening's escapade. I asked what he intended. He said he planned for us to burgle the home of that evening's guest speaker at the public meeting from which we had been so unceremoniously ejected.

Jack was against this.

JACK: You're an idiot, man. Leave well alone. You're just getting your own back.

ROBBY: I'm not asking you, deserter. I'm telling. Either join in or push off.

JACK: You never give up, do you!

ROBBY: Look, you copped out once tonight. Do it again and that's it. Okay?

JACK: So it's a test for me now as well, is it?

ROBBY: You treat it how you like. You know the score.

Their animosity was undisguised. I was not able then to untangle all that lay behind the exchange; this only became clear later, as you will discover in due time.

I was not, of course, myself happy about the proposal. When I voiced my unease, Robby delivered a somewhat lengthy diatribe, of which the following is an abridged version, reproduced as accurately as memory allows in Robby's own words:

'Look, this man is a socialist, right? And supposed to be a champion of the working class, at least that's what he's always claiming. He goes on endlessly about equality and the capitalist oppression and about a fairer distribution of wealth. He shouts about workers' control, nationalization of all the means of production and the institutions of business. You know the kind of stuff, you hear it every day. I believe it, as it happens. Not the slogany side of it, not the bandwaggoneers. I can't stand them any more than that collection of time-servers you saw tonight. But do you know how this paragon of socialist action lives? Eh? He has a house worth upwards of sixty thousand quid, he's got shares in half-a-dozen well-heeled companies and the last thing he'd want is for any happy band of workers to tell him what he's got to do. In other words, he's like all the rest, all he wants is a big slice of whatever there is going. He's a manipulator, that's all, and he mouths socialist doctrine because that's what he knows he has to do to get where he wants to be. It's the fashionable philosophy. You know how he got where he is? Good degree from respectable university. Into a trade union. Organized a nice little strike that he managed to keep going long enough to get sympathetic publicity but not so long that he lost it. From that straight into the national office as a blue-eyed boy. Then a quick side-step into the political corridors at Westminster and bingo, before you know it he's on TV all the time, he's advising unions about companies and employers about trade unions, he's all set for Parliament and is doing all right thank you out of fees, journalism, union support, sinecure salaries and kick-backs. Four hundred years ago he'd have gone into the church, written a classy book on ecclesiastical authority or burned a few heretics and been made a bishop in double-quick time. Bit of sex on the side, not mattering which sort, good food, nice house, secure job. And power. That as much as anything. Status, influence, authority, money. That's the name of the game. Always was, still is. His politics aren't a philosophy and they aren't a mission. And he's not crackers. His politics are a business, a career that gets him what he wants—being one of the elect of the earth.'

As this monologue went on, Robby showed many of the signs of stress which you, Morgan, as a budding M.D. would have been interested to note. He began trembling with anger, his voice became proclamatory as if he were addressing a public meeting. He broke into a sweat, beads of perspiration winked on his forehead, reflecting the firelight. By the end I knew I was watching a fanatic promoting his cause. If the sittingstanding talking man would have done well as a corrupt bishop, Robby would have matched him as a ruthless officer in the department of the inquisition. It was the kind of outburst you cannot reply to; and you cannot politely dismiss or change the subject afterwards.

There was a pause. Robby recovered his composure. (I realized then, watching him, that the thing I had felt vaguely about him all day and had not been able to pin down was that all the time he was on the edge of hysteria, that somehow this was part of both his attractiveness and unattractiveness. Like watching a bomb to see when it might explode. There was rumbling violence always just under the surface of his skin. And I could not

84

tell just at that moment what caused it. I was soon to discover.)

I said, as calmly and as amenably as I could—as though humouring a madman!—that though what he had said was no doubt true, I could not understand why he wanted to burgle the man's house.

I had, he replied, entirely missed the point. Words were no longer enough. Actions were what counted. Only actions revealed intentions truthfully. This man said he was a socialist but acted like any other grabber. This showed his true beliefs. He claimed to believe in equality, in fair distribution of wealth, and to be against greed and privilege. Okay, let him live by that. And as he had so much more than most people let us take some of his unequal wealth and redistribute it. Obviously he would not willingly allow us to do this, so it must be done by a people's tax, by an act on behalf of the people which we, representatives of the people, would execute.

DITTO: I agree with your theory. But not with the action you want to take.

ROBBY: You're a fool, then.

DITTO: Talk sense or not at all.

ROBBY: Okay. You're naive. You've swallowed all that junk they serve up at school about being a good citizen. You're allowing your upbringing to condition you to the morality of the status quo. Just what the cruds want.

DITTO: Crap. I'm saying that if you go around burgling people's houses,

You will have noticed, Morgan, that one of the difficulties of attempting to set down such an account as I am here engaged upon is to reveal simultaneous thoughts and feelings, with concurrent words and actions in such a way that you, dear reader, accept them as being at one, in the moment. Paralleling, as it were, the conversational exchange set down opposite I experienced an interior monologue of influential effect on my decision regarding Robby's criminal suggestion. What he proposed touched, not my mind, but my emotions. My nerves not my thoughts. You

85

however you justify it, it won't be long before everybody is at it whenever they feel like getting something for nothing. And that means nobody comes off best. Certainly not the ordinary bloke, who always comes off worst anyway.

ROBBY: You've no proof that that will happen.

DITTO: Don't talk stupid. It's human nature.

ROBBY: Human nature isn't absolute. It can be changed. And it is changed by conditions.

DITTO: And when your Great Socialist Society finally dawns, there'll be no need to burgle, I suppose.

ROBBY: That's right. Need makes burglars. And there'll be no need.

DITTO: Meanwhile, mayhem on the way to the Great Day.

ROBBY: If necessary, yes.

DITTO: And hard luck on the innocent victims.

ROBBY: To start with, no one is innocent in this fight. Second off, you can't make a cake without

know, Morgan, how often we have inveighed against the narrow restrictions of our education. How we have attacked, between ourselves and to our teachers, the false assumptions made about what we must do in life, how we shall—indeed *must*—live. How we have discussed the possible ways of breaking from that strait-jacket and of reforming it so that others who follow after are not subjected to similar pressures. (Robby was not alone in possessing hotly held ideals!)

I thought, at the same time, of my father, whose whole life has been lived by an honest regard for, a belief in the very system that makes it so that now he lies ill and has for two years suffered for simple want of the means of ease, want of the kind of attention that would alleviate him.

Solemn thoughts; telling emotions. But I have to admit that most persuasive of all was an irrational desire to chance my arm. I wanted to commit a dangerous act, wanted to know what excitements were to be had in crime, wanted for a smashing eggs. Third off, there's no gain without sacrifice, no healing of this sick man without deep surgery. Fourth off, I'm fed up with all this bloody chat. Are you coming or aren't you? Or are you like the rest of them, all hot air? night to play the outlaw. Had I not set out to take indiscriminately what life offered? Could I turn away because it offered something that might offend a delicate sensibility? Of course not. And I knew then what a ghastly tyranny both causes and logic can be.

I said, 'Let's get cracking.'

Jack said, 'You're mad, both of you.'

Robby said, 'Who asked? And who cares whether you come or not?'

Jack said, 'I'm coming, but just to see the kid gets into no trouble.'

Robby said, 'How touching! Or have you yet?'

I said, 'Look, pack it in, you two. If we're going to do it let's go now before I change my crazy mind.'

Robby said, 'We're about a quarter of a mile from the house. We'll leave the car where it is and walk. All we pinch is a few things, valuable, small, resaleable and light. I know just the stuff and I know where it is, so leave the selection to me.'

Scenes From a Burglary

I need hardly remind you, Morgan, that I am not exactly accustomed to burgling houses. True, when climbing up and down my ladder during my Saturday stints of window-cleaning, I have sometimes imagined what burgling a house at night might be like, how I might do it, with what stealth and cunning I would execute the operation—never of course being caught or leaving behind one tell-tale clue to betray my identity. I would even vary my *modus operandi*, thereby foxing the police, whose routine minds would fruitlessly look for a pattern in case after unsolved case.

87

But such idle fantasy was no more than pastime speculation, self-hero daydreaming, a hedge against the boredom of polishing vertical glass hour on hour.

This was to be the real thing.

As we walked up the dark lane away from the river, sweat rashed my body.

I am a fool, I thought. What am I doing here?

Was this a dream? A sleeping fantasy too really felt? A nightmare? I had had a hard day, an unusual day; I was not myself; was sleeping without rest.

But I knew it was not so. I had felt similar symptoms before. While going to the dentist to have a broken tooth pulled. While walking to school for examinations. Most recent and vividly of all, while in the ambulance with my father.

Not a dream. Just fear.

I was scared.

My body did not move as it normally does. An act of will was required. I had to make myself walk. Had to monitor myself, as an engineer monitors a faulty engine, making certain I walked toward this unknown house with apparently normal ease, revealing none of my alarm to my accomplices.

But fear itself is a heady excitement.

*

When we reached the house, large glooming in the nightlight dark, solid (how much more solid than in daylight!), forbidding, Robby put up a hand to stop us in our stride as if he were a marine commando in some wartime raid behind enemy lines.

Fear is also a stimulating fantasist.

*

'Round the back there is an unlocked window that lets into the kitchen,' Robby whispered, we huddled head-to-head.

'How do you know?' I asked.

88

'I drummed the place today,' Robby said.

'O, god!' Jack said, derisive, and muffled an unrepentant guffaw.

*

Gravel crunches like boiled sweets when you crush them in your mouth with senseless regard for your teeth. And the noise abraded a sleeping world.

'Keep on the grass, fool!' puled Robby.

*

A house about to be burgled is like an animal being hunted. As you stalk closer, you expect its eyes to open and discover your malign purpose and you, its mouth to growl a warning. You wait for it to stand up and charge away. Or, worse, to charge at you. That a house does none of these things makes it all the more menacing.

'Bloody silly this is, kiddo,' whispered Jack into my face as we stumbled into each other.

*

'Nobody ever pinches me,' said the burglar's wife to her husband.

*

We reached the cliff face of the house itself, fleas clinging against an elephant.

'The window is to our left,' Robby murmured. 'Edge that way slowly.'

My feet trod soft soil.

'We're in a flowerbed,' I said. 'Leaving footprints!'

'Shut it!' Robby said. 'Who cares?'

89

'The police will care, that's who.'

Jack's mouth to my ear, lips tickling as he said, 'There'll be no police, Sunshine.'

'Optimist,' I whispered.

*

The soles of my feet were tingling in an electrically shocking way. My legs were freeze-dried jelly.

I had felt this before only in one kind of place: when looking down a deep, steep drop, like a precipice or over the edge of a high tower.

*

I needed to urinate. Urgently.

*

'This is it,' said Robby, drawing the other two of us close to him, his arms gripping our shoulders. 'This is the window. It's pretty narrow, and high up. But I reckon if Jack bends down and you, kiddo, stand on his back you'll just be able to reach your arm through the ventilator window, open the catch of the window itself, get in, and then open the back door for us.'

> [*And now, for the first time Oliver, well-nigh mad with grief and terror, saw that housebreaking and robbery, if not murder, were the objects of the expedition. He clasped his hands together, and involuntarily uttered a subdued exclamation of horror. A mist came before his eyes; the cold sweat stood upon his ashy face; his limbs failed him; and he sank upon his knees.*
>
> *'Get up!' murmured Sikes, trembling with rage, and drawing the pistol from his pocket; 'Get up, or I'll strew your brains upon the grass.'*

90

'O! for God's sake let me go!' cried Oliver; 'let me run away and die in the fields. I will never come near London; never, never! O! pray have mercy on me, and do not make me steal. For the love of all bright Angels that rest in Heaven, have mercy upon me!'

The man to whom this appeal was made, swore a dreadful oath, and had cocked his pistol, when Toby, striking it from his grasp, placed his hand upon the boy's mouth, and dragged him to the house.

'Hush!' cried the man; 'it won't answer here. Say another word, and I'll do your business myself with a crack on the head. That makes no noise, and is quite as certain, and more genteel. Here, Bill, wrench the shutter open. He's game enough now, I'll engage. I've seen older hands of his age took the same way, for a minute or two, on a cold night.'

Sikes, invoking terrific imprecations upon Fagin's head for sending Oliver on such an errand, plied the crowbar vigorously, but with little noise.]

'Are you listening?'

'You mean, I've got to go in first?' I said.

'That's it.'

'Now look, Robby,' Jack said.

'Knock it off!' Robby snapped. A threat, no doubt of it. Then, temperate, 'He'll manage. Won't you, kiddo? All experience, eh?'

'I'm out of my tiny mind,' I said.

'Isn't everybody?' Robby said.

*

Q. What did the burglar give his wife for Christmas?
A. A stole.

*

'Why don't you go first? You said you'd looked the place over.'

'Know it like the back of my hand. But I can't reach the window catch. My arm isn't long enough. There's a door just to the left of the window. Open it. One bolt and a Yale. All you do is slip them quietly and we're in.'

'I won't be able to see a damn thing in there. What if I knock over something in the dark? What if there's a dog?'

'There's no dog, and I've got a torch. Just by chance! Here.'

*

There was a poore man on a tyme, the whiche vnto theues, that brake into his house on nyght, he sayde on this wyse: syrs, I maruayle, that ye thynke to fynde any thyng here by nyght: for I ensure you I can fynd nothing, whan it is brode day.
By this tale appereth playnly
That pouerte is a welthy mysery.

*

Other people's houses exude their own smell. House odour. This one smelt of my own armpit fear. My entrance into it was a violation.

*

'The stuff we want is through here,' Robby said, taking the torch from me as he came through the door, and leading the way with alarming lack of caution.

*

A comfortable room. Thick-pile carpet. Big, enfolding chairs. High-polished dark oak antique furniture. A wall of books. Ornaments, knick-knacks, many, the kind you do not touch without feeling the depth of your ignorance and the shallowness of your pocket.

I wanted more than anything to cry out, to shout, 'You are being done!'

*

'Grab this,' said Robby, plunging into my involuntary hands a book, leather bound.

'What is it?'

'A book.'

'Fool. What book?'

'*Das Kapital.*'

'Karl Marx.'

'Educated creep.'

'Why?'

'English edition, 1887. Rare. Worth nearly two hundred quid. Maybe more. Not traceable to present owner. Savvy?'

'Very symbolic!'

'That too.'

'Stop arsing about,' Jack said. 'Get on with it.'

'The trouble with you, Jack,' said Robby, 'is that you've no imagination.'

*

Robby's hand, cadaverous in the torchlight, reached for a luxury china vase, splendid on the high oak mantel of the fireplace, picked it up. Held it.
slipped/dropped
on to the stone flags of the firehearth
like chippings on a grave
A blaze of shiversound.

*

93

'You dropped that flaming thing on purpose!' Jack said out of the shock.

'Rubbish!' Robby said.

There was a scuffle-movement: Jack and Robby together.

The torch dived to the floor. Extinguished.

'You want to be caught! That's it, isn't it!'

'Sod off!'

Jack said, 'Where are you, kid?'

'Here,' I said, the word all but choked.

Jack said, 'We're getting out, quick.'

Stumbling, furniture-blocked steps towards the door.

When the door opened.

Room lights arrested us.

He stood, framed in the doorway, the sittingstanding talking man. At once, sober now, I knew why I had felt I had seen him before.

!! Zap !!

We were burgling Robby's own father.

We were burgling Robby's home.

I'd been a fool.

Again.

And fooled.

Meet the twentieth century's Olympic champion dumdum. The world's prize turniphead.

The light dawned. *Pow!*

Too late.

GazZamWamZap.

Pappatalk

'And what, may I ask, have we here?' Mr Hode said. 'What little party game is this? May I join in?'

We none of us replied, but stood like small boys caught scrumping. As we were. Robby's mouth was bleeding at a corner. Had Jack hit him?

94

Hode looked at each of us in turn. Robby. Jack. Myself. His eyes brooked no brazen stare. He came to me. Took the book from my unresisting hands, examined it as if for damage.

'Herr Marx,' he said. 'More talked about than read. What was your intention, young man?'

He gave me no time to answer, even had I been able to find my voice.

'Never mind. The question is purely rhetorical since you cannot stay.'

I glanced at Jack, who nodded peremptorily towards the door.

Robby was still unmoving, his face an agony of anger frustrated by filial embarrassment. I recognized that look at once, I had felt it so often myself. But was this really how one appeared at such times? So peevishly crushed, so lacking in control? So ugly? Just as I recognized the look on Robby's face, the whole gripped-in stance of his tense body, so I knew too that inside he was a seething confusion of feelings and thoughts: resentment and self-pity and a desperate but ineffective desire to hurt, yet, at the calm centre of his being, also wishing that none of this were so. Wanting, longing even, for it to end. Regretful that his father and himself had come to such a pass. Had Jack been right? Had the accident with the vase been a Freudian slip, or a deliberate act? Whichever, it had a necessary purpose: to get Robby (and us too?) caught.

All along Robby had known how this would end, had willed it to end this way, no matter how he might try to convince himself, as he would, that it had not been so. I knew because I had done the same, and had now to admit it to myself. Standing there in the sullen silence of that unfamiliar room I could admit it to myself, if yet to no one else. Looking at the tortured figure by the cold fireplace made any further self-deception impossible . . . Undesirable.

(It might seem strange to you, reading this, that these thoughts should strike me at that moment. It seems strange to me now too, writing them down. But they did, though as a flash of insight rather than in the linear logic of printed words in

95

neat procession across a page.)

All day I had felt drawn to Robby. I had not been able to resist that underskin of violent energy, that blush of fanatic charm. But in this same instant of insight, fascination vanished as mysteriously and as rapidly as it had seized me. In that second Robby had shown me myself.

Was it cruel selfishness, an ugly weakness in me (another?!) that at this same second I lost all interest in him? Whether it was so or not, I must confess that I did. I knew him, you see, what he was and why he was. All sorts of jigsaw moments from our day together fell now into place, and I knew him. Besides, too much of what I now understood spoke to me about myself, reflected me as if I were looking in a mirror. Perhaps my abrupt loss of interest was an act of self-defence as much as of selfishness? I acted to save myself while there was still time; I could not help but sense that Robby was already lost.

'You can find your own way out, I take it?' said Mr Hode. He turned to Jack. 'I think you too had better leave, Jack. I'm sure you would not want to overstay your welcome. Do call and pick up your things another day, if you'd rather.'

'Turn him out and I go as well. For good,' said Robby, clench-mouthed and still unmoving.

His father did not take his eyes from Jack. 'I think Robby and I ought to discuss matters in private, if you wouldn't mind, Jack.'

'You heard me,' said Robby.

There was a moment's silence. Tense. A fulcrum. Whatever was to be done had to be done now. Afterwards would be too late. A private war and a private peace turned on this point in time.

Jack sighed. 'I'm going, Robby,' he said. 'It's best. There's nowt now, you know that.'

'I'm glad you're being sensible,' said Hode.

'Sensible!' shouted Robby. 'O, Christ!' He turned and sat, hunched, in a chair that flanked the fire, dabbing a hand at his bleeding mouth.

'Well?' said Hode to Jack and myself.

Our final cue to leave. But despite my loss of interest in Robby, I felt a twinge of guilt at leaving him to such defeat. Not he himself, but he anyone.

'Perhaps we should talk all this over together?' I said with pale conviction.

Hode rounded on me. 'Young man,' he said, 'I do not know who you are, nor why you are here. But I saw the trouble you helped cause tonight, and that is enough for me. As far as I am concerned you have no business in this house, nor is there anything I wish to discuss with you. You may leave now, or I shall call the police and have you charged with breaking and entering. Which shall it be?'

One of the worst things about being our age is the way an adult like Hode can beat you down with words—or me anyway; I expect you, Morgan, would have withstood him. Your only answer—mine anyway—is either to stand there flabbergasted or to lash out in uncontrolled anger and make an idiot of yourself. This time I was reduced to an angry flabbergast. From which Jack rescued me.

'How-way, kiddo,' he said. 'Let's go.'

Nightcap

Outside the night was frosty. I realized I was lathed in sweat, was flushed.

We paused in the road, the moon shining through the leaves of overhanging trees, brindling the surface.

'What now?' I said, feeling suddenly lost. Abandoned. Empty. Shock, I suppose, after the excitements.

'I'm going to doss down in the shed at work,' Jack said. 'It's just down the road a bit. There's some sacks and we could brew up on the stove. Want to come?'

I had heard him; but my mind was still catching up.

'What gets me,' I said sullensick, 'is that all the time he was just using me.'

97

Jack laughed, a sound like the call of a preying night bird.
'O, aye?' he said.

'Well, wasn't he?' I said, defiant.

'Aye, I suppose he was.'

'You know he was. He was planning it with you all along, from when we were in the pub at lunch time.'

'Yes. I didn't know all the details. But I knew the kind of thing it was likely to be.'

'And you didn't warn me.'

Jack said nothing; gazed at me in the moongloom.

'All right,' I said, 'so he was your mate.'

'And you were like a rabbit spelled by a fox. Even if I'd told you, you'd still have done what he wanted.'

He was right, I knew.

'Maybe. But it was the way he used me that gets my gut.'

'So he used you, Sunshine. What were you doing?'

'What d'you mean?'

'He used you, sure. But you must have been using him. And me an'all.'

Experience. It's all experience.

'How do you know what I was doing?'

That bird of prey laugh again.

'Because everybody is using everybody else all the time, kiddo. We're all users. That's what people *are*.'

Why did I laugh? For I did. And felt myself again. Almost refreshed, even if tired. Very tired.

'You're a cynic, Jack, you know that?'

'I know I'm nowt of the sort. Now are you coming with me or not?'

It would have been another experience; but I could not. It was too much. Like everything else, it seems, you can have too much experience for one day.

'No thanks, Jack, not tonight.'

'I can promise you a good time.'

'I'll see you around, eh?'

'I hope, bonny lad.'

'What'll you do now?'

'Hang about Richmond for a day or two, just in case Robby . . . But he won't. It's done.'

'And if it is?'

'I'll move on somewhere. Dunno where. Doesn't matter. There's always sommat wherever you go.' That laugh again.

'So long then.'

'So long. Take care. Sunshine.'

He turned and walked away up the moonspeckled road, a slight figure in that chequered light, despite his bulk. His feet made no sound. He might have been a ghost.

When he was out of sight, I walked back down the lane towards the river and Robby's car where I had left my pack. I thought of spending the night there, where we had sat earlier.

As I turned to go, there came from the Hodes' house the sound of voices raised in argument. I could not make out what was being said, only the hard, brutal clash of anger. Nor could I distinguish son's voice from father's. They were as one sound, one voice, like a man battling against himself.

THE LEAP

How to set this down? How to describe it? It happened to me,
but not me. I was him, but not him. Haven't you, Morgan,
ever been through a day when you were not yourself? When it
was not you who experienced your events but some other you?
This day was like that for me. So how to describe it and make
you believe how it was, how it seemed? How to show you
me-him this day?

Begin at the beginning. As I-I. As eye.

Slept solidly. A cuckoo woke me. Unexpectedly refreshed.
Fit. Healthy. Happy, I suppose. (How do you ever know?
What's the proof?) Optimistic, certainly; full of energy. And
hungry. Yet, as I say, not quite myself. Somehow other.

A bright day. Crystal light glaze-blinking the tingle-crisp
river, where I plunged myself, in-out, quickish. Naked. Like
the day. Skin-sizzling afterwards.

Yesterday seemed a shaggy dog story. Had it been? Why
bother to wonder? Why consider? Consideration is for recollec-
tion in Wandsworth. (The day's first terrible witticism. Apologies. The crazed light made my brain flippant.)

Packed pack. On back. Strode into Richmond. There: break-
fasted—bacon, egg, sausage, beans, toast, marmalade, tea, tea,
tea, tea (I was bottomlessly thirsty), tea. At Johnny's Cafe
(truly!).

'Why not just buy the urn, love,' said the busty waitress,
bodied as undulatory as the dales, at my sixth request. 'Where
you putting it all? Softens the brain, too much tannin.'

'Not to mention its deleterious effects on other parts,' I said.

'Cheeky,' she said, unflurried. 'An early bird. Have you
shaved yet?'

'No, does it excite you?'

She rubbed her hand, lascivious, down my jaw. 'Know what I would do?'

'What's that?'

'Put some milk on and let cat lick it off.'

'Ah, well,' I said. 'You can't win 'em all. Thought maybe you liked them young.'

She put my bill down on the counter. 'Chicken, I like them any age, but I'm busy just now.'

A nymphomaniac waitress! A narrow escape!

Time to make a quick getaway before she rips off her pinny and assaults me on the prepacked bacon in her storecupboard.*

A limbering up for Helen! Which reminds me, where's the telephone? Outside Woolies.

Riffle through the telephone book (cigarette-smokey-sniffy, dogeared pages, scrawled messages, e.g. *Come and lay me, cooky 3694758. Tringaling my dingaling 6256943.*) And I'm away.

Hello?

Could I speak to Helen, please?

Just a minute, the baby's crying.

I'm sorry, that's better.

Could I speak to Helen, please?

O, yes, just a minute, who shall I say?

Tell her, it's the boy she left behind.

It's who . . . the baby's crying again. Just a minute . . . Helen! . . .

---

*The worst case of unexpected sex education I have so far heard of was told me by Simon Feldman, who claimed that Lisa Pringle, whose father was an undertaker, trapped him in the workshop behind her father's office one Saturday afternoon, backed him into an upright coffin and there molested him. Had the coffin not been de luxe lined, Simon said, he did not think he would have survived the ordeal, which has understandably left him with a strong prejudice against undertakers, whose profession he was at one time considering as a career because, he said, as an undertaker he would never be out of work.

She's just coming.

Hello?
Help.
O!
Pee.
It's you.
Go to the top of the class and give the penicillin out.
You're chirpy.
Cheeky, I've just been told.
That too. By whom?
Waitress in Richmond where I purchased sustenance.
And anything else?
She was too busy.
Not that you weren't willing.
No. She was a little Massy Harris for my taste.
Have you any?
Can you have, without experience to teach discrimination?
Always one for the words.
The currency of intercourse. I thank you for the compliment.
Take it how you like.
You're still mad at me?
Am I?
I'm asking.
I'm wondering.
Words it was did for me yesterday, eh?
Perhaps.
I'm sorry.
Are you?
I think so. Will you forgive me?
I'm not sure.
If I say please?
I don't like being called . . .
Promiscuous?
Yes.
You knew the word.

Yes.

Ah, I see! You can't talk?

No.

The baby's stopped crying.

Yes.

We could conduct this conversation much more comfortably somewhere else. This phone box stinks.

I'm not sure I want to.

Look, Helen, I meant what I said on that note.

Embarrassing!

At the bus?

Yes.

Desperation breeds disregard. But I'm sorry if I embarrassed you.

Two apologies in one day. What's the world coming to!

Never mind the world. What about us?

Whatever have you been doing, watching old movies?

Nothing so exciting. What have you been doing, by the way?

Nothing so exciting.

You too? We must meet at once and swap notes.

As they say.

But I am—desperate, I mean.

For what?

Do you want the graphic details on the telephone? We might be bugged.

All right. Don't bother.

You'll meet me?

What'll you do if I don't?

Throw myself off Richmond Castle into the Swale?

Not imaginative enough.

Streak through Gunnerside at tea time on Sunday?

There's nothing you've got that they haven't seen here in abundance. Boring. Anyway, most of them here are Primitive Methodists.

And you've not had any excitement? Tut, tut. Well, let me see. Dress in drag as a district nurse, call on your aunt saying I've come at the request of her visiting niece to check her for pregnancy.

You've a putrid mind.

Desperation, as they say, knows no squalor.

Okay, where?

The 11.44 from Reeth, arriving Hag Wood by the caravan site 12.10. I'll be waiting in the bushes disguised as a weary rambler.

All right but under protest.

Protest as much as you like, but give in in the end.

Anyway, how did you find this number?

Elementary, my dear Watsonia. Your uncle's your dad's brother. So much I knew. Your dad's brother is likely to own the same surname as your dad. And therefore yours. A quick ogle at the invaluable GPO reference manual. Three are listed. Only one in Gunnerside. Bingo.

Smarty pants.

See you.

If you behave yourself.

O, and Helen . . .

What?

Don't bother to bring your pyjamas.

The town was busying. I wanted to leave before anyone who had been at last night's fracas recognized me. This town ain't big enough for both of us. But I had things to buy. I wanted everything right for Helen.

The food was easy. Brown rolls, still warm from the oven; lettuce, cos—the crispy kind; a couple of soused herring for starters. Two fresh-cooked meat pies with flaky pastry from Fawcetts and a small tub of sauerkraut (we'd have to pig it with our fingers) for seconds. A quarter of Wensleydale cheese, a couple of pears for afters.

But what to drink? Beer was the obvious thing. But cans are bulky and weigh heavy and I was already overloaded. I had had to tie a plastic bag containing the food on to my pack. So I settled for a couple of large McEwans and set off out of the square, making for the High Gingerfield road out of town, up on to Out Moor above Whitcliffe Scar. But I was not happy about the drink. There was not enough and beer was the expected thing.

In Victoria Road I passed Saccone and Speed, the wine shop. *Voilà!* In I went.

I know nothing about wine. I would like to. What little I've drunk I've liked. But wine is another case of plenty of indiscriminate experience being needed to breed discriminate taste.

At those prices, who can drink enough of the stuff ever to know?

Enter a grey-suited middled-aged gent of retired military appearance. An imbiber. Sharp, red veins laced his face.

'Sir?'

Pointless to prevaricate; he would know. Bull by horns.

'I know nothing about wine. But I would like a reasonably priced bottle that would go well with a picnic. Could you suggest anything?'

'I'll do my best. Of course, it all depends on your preference —your palate, you know. And on the food.'

'I don't know what I prefer. But the food is soused herring, meat pie, and Wensleydale.'

His eyes scanned the shelves. Soldier bottles on parade, labels at the present. Some flat out.

'With the meat and cheese, I'd suggest this.'

A baby laid in my dubious hands.

'A youngish Côte du Rhone. Not too heavy. Nothing special but a pleasant wine that can stand a little . . . ill treatment.' A laugh. 'If you'll pardon the presumption.'

'I'll take it, thanks.'

I was left with a pound by the time I'd paid for the bottle, which cost me as much as all the food put together.

'You have a corkscrew, sir?'

'On my knife.'

'Could I suggest? Allow me to open the bottle for you. I'll replace the cork securely but leaving enough for you to pull it out when you're ready. And, if I might advise, I would remove the cork a couple of hours before drinking. Let the wine breathe, you understand. It will taste all the better. Not left in the glare of the sun, but not kept cold.' He eyed my pack as he disgorged the cork. 'And keep it upright as near as conditions allow.'

'I'll do my best. Thanks for the help.'

Laugh again. 'Delighted. I'll just tuck the bottle into this side pocket, shall I? Safe there, and upright. You shouldn't have any trouble. Just be careful when you dismount.'

We enjoyed his joke together this time.

'Have a good picnic. Wish I was going with you myself. Lovely day for it.'

Off up Hurgill Road and Belleisle Hill at a steady plodding pace, in high spirits. The morning—nine thirty by now—still spring-brisk enough to make walking with a loaded pack pleasant work. As I slowly left behind the last houses of the town, rising above them till Richmond itself was a cluster below, I felt again as I always do going up into the dale an almost explosive sense of release, of unfettering freedom. Like leaving a hot, stuffy room crowded with people, and stepping out into an elevated garden laid out in sparely planted folds that carry you up, one beyond another, always one more beyond, into the stretching sky. Earth breakers surfing you on to the skylimitless shore of space.

I love highpoints of unbroken landview. I love carved cliffs, scooped valleys, distant rivers mirroring the sky.

> *Whitcliffe Wood and Scar.*—Towards the west end of town, through Quaker Lane, is the *West Field*, a beautiful open walk full of delightful prospects, which succeed each other in endless variety; and at the upper end of it, is *Whitcliffe Wood*, and the frightful precipice called *Whitcliffe Scar*, 'where,' to use the words of Mr. Clarkson, 'we see the violent convulsions which the surface of this globe must have received at the great deluge, when the earth was torn from its centre, and

rocks, water, and woods, separated from their old habitations, were removed to a distance.' On ascending the bold romantic Scar, we behold the wild and sublime rocks projecting on every side, and wooded to the very edge of the precipice; and on its summit is a spot known as *Willance's Leap.—History and Topography of the City of York and the North Riding of Yorkshire, Whellam, Vol 2, 1859.*

For Dad it is the sea. The sea and the sky. A ship and a star. His romance. His image of release. His break into space.

At Redcar a flimsy-seeming (to me, fourteen) fishing smack-boat, a cobble, famed for seaworthyness and tough as rawhide. But out we went though weather worrying, wind and waves rolling with white horses on their spines. Into the troughs and seasick rolling with the curling sea above one second and below the next and Dad laughing and handwringing his pleasure, his release, while I groaned and puked and wished for home and still landed fish quick as I could drop my line, one flapping, gasping, scale-glistening, glaze-eyed, musclebound, cold-blooded, fin-spiked, salt-smacking vertebrate after another as though every gill-breathing member of the rollercoasting North Sea swim wanted to join us in that heaving tub, perhaps in order to escape the tide of bile I was pouring into the waves.

But when our pleasure jaunt was over, we back ashore like all jolly sailor lads grinned undaunted courage at our perilous exploit while pitiful landwalkers crowded our ark to buy at knockdown bravado rates the rewards of our daring. And Dad might have been salted Neptune himself as he gazed with longing a last time at the now high-treacherous ocean before we drove inland home.

It was his last time: never again since.

In his hospital bed does he now fancy himself becalmed on a sunless windless sea?

How do I tell you, Morgan, that there, just above High Ginger-field and just below Rasp Bank, I suddenly and without self-warning, wept? I did. Hills and sky before me, sea and sunless bed within my plodding memory met confluent in my flooding eyes and wrecked me. I had to stumble to the road-skirting wall and cling to its cool, crumpled stone for comforting support. And I did not merely weep. I gasped for air like a drowning man, my body clenched in an uncontrollable spasm.

Lamentation for dying boy and dying man.

Subdued, and at last calm, I set off for the Scar, sly-eying around me in case I had been observed. (Why is it we are so ashamed to cry?)

Just by Out Moor radio beacon you cut across quarter of a mile of mirey coarse-grass field, then through a gate, and you are there: on Whitcliffe Scar. The double-monument: one, a square-based obelisk imprisoned in an iron-rod cage; the other, twenty-four feet away and ten feet lower on the slithering valley side, a grave stone, triangle topped. Each inscribed with the same celebratory message.

1606

HEAR US

GLORY BE TO OUR

MERCIFUL GOD

WHO MIRACULOUSLY

PRESERVED ME FROM

THE DANGER SO GREAT

He wishing to be heard was one Robert Willance, a Westmor-land man by birth:

> who had pushed his way to wealth as a draper in Richmond. With his name is connected the following marvellous story, thus told by Canon Raine:—

'In the year 1606 he was hunting near his own estate, on the high ground between Clints and Richmond, on the northern bank of the Swale. The hunting party were surprised by fog, and Willance was mounted upon a young and fractious horse. To his horror it ran away with him, and made right for the precipitous rock called Whitcliffe Scar, which looks down upon the Swale. The horse, no doubt, as it neared the verge would become conscious of its peril; but as is very frequently the case, the danger that paralyses the rider only makes the steed more fearless. As soon as it left the level platform above, three bounds, each covering twenty-four feet, brought it to the verge of the cliff, down which it sprang. About a hundred feet from the top of the scar there is a projecting mass of rock and earth, upon which the horse alighted, only to throw itself upon the ground below, some hundred feet further down. It was killed by the fall, and Willance's leg was broken. With wonderful presence of mind, he disentangled himself from the dead horse, and, drawing a clasp knife, he slit open the belly of the animal, and laid within it his fractured leg, to protect it from the cold till help arrived. This precaution in all probability, saved his life. His leg, however, was amputated, and he would hunt no more. As a memorial to his wonderful escape, he marked with an upright stone each of the three bounds which his steed took before it sprang over the cliff. On two of them he put the following inscription: "1606. Glory to our merciful God, who miraculously preserved me from the danger so great." And he had indeed great cause to be thankful, for no one can look at the grey cliff over which he was carried without a shuddering feeling of astonishment that any one could survive so fearful a fall.'—*History, Topography and Directory of North Yorkshire*, T. Bulmer & Co., 1890.

Willance's Leap on Whitcliffe Scar was to be my riding place too.

My tent-site I already knew: a flat grassy ledge, thirty yards down valley from the monuments, and nicely below eye-level of anyone strolling along the scar edge. From view below it was screened by bushes, yet over which, lying in my valley-facing tent, I could see the inward-curving ribbon of Swale glinting in its bed. Hag Wood rose opposite up the fist of moor ending in a straight edge just below the top, leaving the moor bald headed and grained with a fish-net grid of dry-stone walls. Bluegrey misted hills touched the sky beyond.

My eyrie.

(I say that, but have never wished to be a bird. Cannot say I have ever thought about it, in fact. But it is a good image of my site, and my feeling that day: poised and predatory. Not like an eagle, though; all too grand. More like a modest kestrel.)

Ten-fifty. Only just time to pitch my tent, stow the food behind a keep-cool rock, the wine, uncorked in the shade of my tent-flap, and then a careful scramble down the scar, across the river (hoping the rope bridge was still there, its frayed demise having long been expected) and up through the caravan park to the road in time to meet the 11.44 from Reeth. If the bridge had collapsed at last, I was in for a wet crossing.

Filled my water bottle at the caravan park. Then, early, not late, after all. Ten minutes to spare. Patrolled the road, eyes restless for sign of moving metal-green. Mouth dry. Limbs in a faint tremble. Nerves.

She climbed down. Stockingless feet in open sandals, scruffy-smart blue jeans perfectly faded, smoothly fitting; loose cheese-cloth shirt in subdued stripes of colour, revelatorily tantalizing; long hair, light brown, shampoo bouncy; old patchwork shoulderbag bulging and nonchalantly swung. A desirable cliché.

Ditto stares untongued, not sure how he wishes this adventure to begin now it has begun. Helen stands in the road confronting him, as bus noise and engine fumes vanish into the distant air.

'I can't be so stunning,' says Helen. 'And it would be nice to leave this road in case we're seen. . . . I said I was going shopping . . .'

There was a moment when he might say goodbye.

But it passes.

He smiles, feeling a corncob boy.

'Stunning!' He hopes his tone displays his doublemeaning mind. Pointing to the road at their feet, he says, 'From here.' He raises his arm, straightstiff, slowly, till pointing finger directs Helen's eyes to the no more than nipple-point of Willance's caged obelisk intruding into the sky, 'To up there.'

'Hmm,' she says. 'Quite a stretch.'

'A vertical stroll to give you an appetite for lunch. May I take madam's bag?'

They saunter off towards the river, through the bungaloid urban order of the caravan park, affecting casual uninterest in the face of curious caravaners ogling Helen.

The slewing rope bridge brings the first shedding of pretence.

'I can't cross *that*!' she says. 'It's crazy!'

'Fairground fun,' he says. 'Here, grab my hand. Just swing with it, don't fight it. Bend at the knees. And don't look at the water.'

She is giggling with excitement and has lost her magazine-phony sophistiwalk. Like a bather testing the water, she treads suspiciously on to the footboards of the slippery bridge. Her laughter clams into eager concentration and he sees her prettier self. Stepping backwards that he might face her and give her reassurance, he thinks how self-forgetfulness brings out the beautiful in people.

They reach the middle. Low point, they are but ten feet above the river, the bridge swaying its dizzying worst. He makes her pause.

'It's so scarey!' she says but with confidence now. Her speaking is almost drowned in the riversurge. She hazards releasing his hand to push back her hair from curtaining her face, where the breeze has blown it. But grabs again as she loses balance. He finds enjoyment in her dependence. He squeezes her hand and she smiles with all her face through the veiling hair, eyes and mouth confirming the truth of the shared moment.

'You get a smashing view from here,' she shouts.

Their heads turn. Suspended above the water, they see the river sweeping into perspectives, trees and bushes and rocks serrating the lines of its banks; and the valley rising beyond. Nowhere else, he thinks, can you feel the river's energy, its own life, as here. From the bank it seems almost placid, certainly contained and gentle. From here you knew it for what it was, maker of the valley, a powerful force. Here you knew the river did not belong to the dale but the dale to the river. Swale's dale.

'Ready?' he asked when they had looked their fill, and the bridge had settled its thrashing. She nodded and with surer feet they climbed the slope to the bank.

On firm ground again, she exhaled her tension and looked back across the poppling ropes.

'Mmm,' she crooned her satisfaction.

He turned and led the way, zig-zagging up the backbending slope, and then on to the wall of the scar, finding footholds and a safe path for her.

They trudge, she two paces behind him, for ten minutes without pause or word. A steady plod is his way with steep hills; but he admires her perseverance and uncomplaining willingness to follow his lead. Occasionally he glances back at her. Each time her head comes up, as though she is waiting for him to look at her, and she smiles. Soon her face glistens with so fine a sweat she seems to glow. The sight of her like that, warm, her loose shirt clinging now so that he can see the shape and movement of her breasts, stirs in him a desire he has not yet felt that day. He begins to tremble again, this time almost uncontrollably, and dares not look back at her again till the emotion has worn to an ache of anticipation. He can hardly wait to reach the top, to be with her in his secluding tent, and has to restrain himself from increasing the pace of their ascent. All the time he wants to turn and hold her under pretext of helping her safely over some sup-posedly difficult ground. But he resists that urge too, fancying she will detect his real motive for touching her and reject him, something he knows will embarrass him; worse, she might tease his crude duplicity.

(All this was in my mind—and body—as I climbed. But much more at the same time. As I climbed and lusty desires climbed in me, I also thought and felt much more in parallel, so to speak, and in a reasonless stream. Like:

the pleasurable exertion in bone and muscle pushed to the point of pain

which led me to dwell for a minute or two on how often pain and pleasure are but a hairline apart—is sexual pleasure painful too?—as are sanity and madness, laughter and hysteria, hate, they say, and love

but even while these thoughts and sensualities occupied me, I was aware that my pants were snarling my testicles and hitched my jeans to release myself from discomfort

I worried about my feet for a while: would they smell if/when I took off my boots? I'd have to take off my boots, wouldn't I? Would FO put her off? An ironic chuckle had to be suppressed into a cough

rabbit droppings, like raisins, lying in the spikey moorgrass sent my eyes searching for burrows and my mind turning over snatches of Midge holding forth on the theme 'Is *Watership Down* a fascist book?'—he thought yes on the whole and argued undeniably as Midge always does, only Sayers challenging him, as on such occasions Sayers always does

needed to urinate but decided I could wait till we reached the top

suddenly without clue I thought of Robby and Jack. Yesterday seemed a dream away, yet vividly present so that my stomach lurched as if I had suffered a shock, even a blow. 'We're all users,' Jack had said. Me too now, I wondered. And Helen? Of course

would the wine be okay? Would she think it pretentious? Silly?

dad, I wondered about, felt guilty about because I had not telephoned today. But pushed from my mind

Even to list these things like this is to suggest they came in sequence and order. It was not so: they were random, scrambled, disordered. Everybody's being is like a collage. And a mobile. A multimovement of circumsensethoughts. And no one can ever record them all, not at once, or singly, or ever. All literature is incomplete history.

> history is a pattern
> Of timeless moments.

[T. S. Eliot, you'll remember, Morgan.]

So why do we try, why do we make the certainly hopeless effort to record our experience? Why do I? Now, here, on this hillside, and here on this white paper? Because [T.S.E. again]

> each venture
> Is a new beginning, a raid on the inarticulate

?

Or just because there is nothing better to do? Or nothing to do that's a better way of spending the time between birth and death?

I thought all this too, on the scar as we climbed.)

We reached the graveyard monument to Willance's survival and flopped gratefully down, side by steaming side, our backs against Willance's cooling stone, our beaming faces drinking the conquered view.

Breath recovered, bodies relaxed, I said:

'Want an epulation?'

Without taking her eyes from the curving dale below she said, 'At it again, word child?'

'Only to confirm my consistency.'

'You know, people at school said you weren't very clever, just a plodder.'

'And?'

'You don't seem exactly birdbrained to me.'

'Does it matter to you, one way or the other?'

'Not really. Brains aren't everything by any means. Just interests me. Does it bother you?'

'It did, when I was about fourteen. Not so much now. I've begun to find my feet a bit. I don't imagine I'm a budding genius, anything stupid like that. But I don't agonize about what people think of me as much as I used to. People at school, I mean.'

'But you do agonize about what some people think of you?'

'Doesn't everyone?'

'I suppose so.'

'Don't you?'

'Maybe.'

'Come on, confess. Why should I be the only one to play at telling secrets?'

'Touché. Yes, all the time.'

'You always seemed so confident to me.'

'You always seemed so standoffish to me.'

'So why the picture and the letter?'

'Can you bear the truth?'

'I can bear honesty. Let's decide afterwards if it's the truth.'

'Brum-brum!'

'Pompous. Sorry.'

'But clever. Exactly what I mean about you. The people who put you down couldn't even have thought it.'

'Thanks. Morgan could.'

'Morgan doesn't put you down.'

'Doesn't he? That surprises me.'

'Then you don't know Morgan very well.'

'I thought I did, but . . .'

'Never mind Morgan, let's get back to us.'

'How about my epulation first?'

'Is it nasty?'

'Soused herring, lettuce, brown rolls. Meat pie and sauer-kraut. Wensleydale. Pears. A bottle of wine.'

'And thou beside me. Sounds like a feast.'

'Exactly.'

'However did you manage it? Up here, I mean.'

'To the pure all things are possible.'

'How much longer do you expect to keep your purity?'

She was looking directly at me, our faces only a shoulder apart.

'As brief a time as I can.'

She leaned to me; kissed me softly on the mouth, unhurried.

'Then we had better eat at once,' she said.

'Each other or my epulation?'

She laughed. 'Stop using that silly word. Your feast will be a good appetiser.'

'I'm not going to say I love you or anything of that sort.'

'It doesn't matter. Just pretend. You think too much.'

'Isn't pretence a lie?'

'Not always,' she said, kissing me again. 'It can just be make-believe.'

'You know a difference?'

'Isn't lying a way of deceiving? It can hurt. Is usually meant to hurt. Yes?'

'Yes, I suppose it is.'

'Moral rape, that's what lying is. But everybody makes believe, don't they? Like children playing. Taking part. Making life how they want it to be, what they wish it was.'

'Pretending life into happening?'

'Exactly. Couldn't have put it better myself.'

'I thought I was supposed to be the clever one.'

'I just let you think so!'

She kissed me again, pushed herself to her feet, laughing.

'I think we should eat,' she said.

There are days when everything goes well, when everything fits. This was one of them. We felt now at ease with each other, happy to be together. The food was tasty, the wine (I silently thanked my grey-suited military adviser) was soft and smooth. We drank beer with the herring to help shift the vinegar and take the edge from our climbers' thirsts. Until we reached the cheese we spoke of nothing but the meal and the view and of Willance and his Leap (I was made to tell the story) and the satisfaction of lounging half-in, half-out of a tent, itself hidden yet providing such a vantage. But this was nothing more than chat, entertaining, but, we both knew, no more than pleasantry before the business of our meeting.

By the end of our leisurely meal the wine was settling the thoughts in my head, leaving me happily drowsy.

Then Helen said, 'Are you fortified against the truth?'

'Against your honesty, I thought we agreed. Lay on, MacDuff.'

'The laying *may* come later.'

'Letter and picture.'

As though preparing for battle, she cleared from around us the detritus of our meal, pushing it into the plastic bag I had carried the food in, and stowing the bundle out of sight behind the wall of the tent. That done, she settled herself on her back, comfortably at my side, her head pillowed by my pack, her long legs stretched out and crossed at the ankles. Through the bushes we could glimpse the curve of the valley bending away: focus for our self-conscious eyes.

'I was bored,' she began, as if telling a story. Something in her tone told me she had carefully rehearsed the words. (So she expected the question and prepared a reply; was I hearing an honest account, after all?) 'You've no idea how much I hate living in the country. The country is lovely for days out,' a lift

of the head, turned to me in proffering manner, 'days like this.'
She leaned toward me, brushing her lips against mine; relaxed
back again. 'But to live in it's ghastly. I'm a town mouse.'

She paused. If I was meant to say something, I could not.
Her deliberate performance amused me but irritated me too
somehow. I stared at the view knowing she would go on.

'One day I was tormenting myself by looking through my old
rubbish. You know, the sort of stuff everyone keeps. Old diaries,
letters, silly mementoes, photographs. Having a wallow down
memory lane. Among the photographs was one of a gang of us
on a school trip to York. D'you remember? Charlie Dawson was
sick in the coach. Susan Parker got lost in the railway museum
—so *she* said, I've my own ideas about that ha ha. Miss Cobbs
was goosed by a verger in the Minster and hit high C. A
reverberation of ecstasy such as those ancient stones had not
echoed in centuries. The line was Midge's, you'll recall. All the
usual stuff. Anyway, I was looking at this photograph and thinking that I'd been out with every boy in it except one.'

Another pause. Another turn of the head, this time displaying
a pert grin.

'You, of course,' she said, lying back again. 'I thought, why
should he be the odd man out? Why should he escape my deadly
charms?' She laughed, self-mocking. 'So I sat down, wrote the
letter, chose a suitable photograph, and sent them off. My
stratagem worked. We're here.'

As though a curtain had dropped at the end of a play, she gave
up her role as storyteller, flopped on to her stomach and stared
into the tent, hands supporting chin.

'D'you believe that?' she asked, the flippantly anecdotal tone
quite gone, replaced by a seriousness that betrayed anxiety.

I thought a moment, not quite sure which direction our conversation was taking.

'Superficially.'

She glanced at me, playful no longer. 'Tell me.'

'It *could* have been like that, but sounded phony the way you
told it.'

'If it *was* like that, would it . . .'

Larks. Breeze-brushed grass and leaves. A question hanging.

'Make any difference now?' I said.

She nodded, face held away, as though expecting a blow.

'We haven't come here under any delusions, have we?' I said. 'It was you who said pretend.'

'I know. Now . . . I'm not sure.'

'What does that mean?'

'I hoped you'd tell me.'

I laughed, finding nothing funny. 'I've problems enough of my own to sort out. Sorry.'

She sat up, cross-legged, facing me. Her fingers picked at the ground between us. She seemed then very vulnerable, very attractive. In a movement too quick and awkward, I laid my hand over hers.

'I'm not sure I can explain,' she said. Taking my hand, she began playing with my fingers, a disturbing pleasure.

'Try,' I said but wishing only to attend to our intimate touching.

'Well, I suppose you're right really. Superficially, that is how it happened. You know—that *was* the plot. My plot. But you know what old Midgely says about plots? Plots . . . what is it?'

Fingertip provocation.

I managed to say, 'Plots more often conceal meaning than reveal it.'

'That's it. What a frightening man he is!'

' "Look behind the action, boy, that's where the true meaning lies." ' Mimicking Midge is my one successful histrionic, as you know, Morgan.

Helen laughed, and bending in her laughter kissed my hand in hers.

'What lies behind your plot, then?' I asked.

'I've been puzzling about that one ever since we were climbing the scar and I realized there was more to my plot than met the eye.'

'And?'

She breathed in deeply and out again, gathering herself for something difficult to say.

'I know I've got a reputation as an easy lay and I play up to it. But boys are shocking boasters. You give them a sweaty grope for five minutes and to hear them talk afterwards you'd think they'd outclassed Casanova. As a matter of fact, I've gone all the way only four times. No more. Honest. Well, four and a half times.'

'And a half!'

She chuckled, her brittle everyday school self breaking through. 'The half was a dishy mutual acquaintance from the first fifteen reputed to be an experienced randy stud, a challenge therefore not to be passed up. He enticed me—so *he* thought—into his room when his parents were out one evening. We were at a point of no return when we heard his mother's voice in the street outside. By then I wasn't in a state to care. But you'd be surprised what a mother's voice can do to a boy!'

We neither of us laughed.

Helen released my hand, turned bodily away, facing the dale.

'I'm sorry. That was cheap.'

'Inappropriate just now, that's all.'

We stared at the distant river; she, no doubt, regretting her words, me regretting the withdrawal of touching hands. For a moment we lost contact.

'I can be cheap,' she said after a while, so quietly I could hardly hear her. 'Loud. You know? Blowsy. Maybe I get my reputation as much because of that as because of anything I . . . do. It's just that there are times when I can't help being . . . I don't know . . .'

'Crude?'

'Yes, not to put too fine a point on it. Bloody crude.'

'Like sometimes wanting to fart in public. Just to shock.'

She laughed and flopped on to her side facing me. Closely.

'You understand.'

'I think so.'

'It's as though two people are inside me, quite different

120

people who have to take it in turns at being me.'

The nearness of her body was intoxicating, like the wine, going to my head. My body tingled with paradoxes. Drowsy yet every cell aware of Helen's warm presence. Relaxed yet trembling for her touch. Unrestrained yet afraid of making the slightest wrong gesture which might break the spell. Careless of meaning and consequence yet anxious for reason and purpose.

'Tell me about your two people,' I said, wishing only to preserve somehow the presence of this moment.

'O,' she said, her eyes avoiding mine, 'one of them is always wanting to go new places, meet new people, do new things. The other is scared of all that, is shy, I suppose, afraid, never sure of herself, not wanting to fail and always feeling she has. One of me is always wanting to break the rules and outrage everybody, especially my parents. That's why I'm crude sometimes and like being thought an easy lay. I started taking the pill just to shock my parents. Or was it because the other one inside me was scared things might go wrong? Because the other one hates upsetting people or getting into trouble.'

'Which one is you now?'

Her eyes found mine and held them with a cool firmness a little frightening in its strength.

'Which one would you prefer?'

I tried to smile, to joke, 'Can't I have both?'

She did not smile in reply. 'I've never tried being both at once before. Is it possible, do you think?'

How could I answer?

Her slim length lay patterning mine so closely I could feel the warmth of her body, yet nowhere touching. My eyes explored her face; her eyes travelled mine. But looking was not enough. I raised my hand, ran my fingertips slowly over her forehead, down the curve of her cheek to the soft firmness of her jaw, round the bow of her chin, up to her lips.

She kissed my fingertips, a sensual caress.

I bent over her, kissed her mouth tentatively, but then, finding eager response, with force. She gripped me to her, pulled my shirt from my jeans, thrust her hand beneath, stroked my back, firmly searching.

Time collapsed, obliterating memory.

Clothes were suddenly an intolerable encumbrance. I plucked impatiently at her flimsy shirt as if it were riveted armour.

'Wait, wait!' she said. A laugh as hasty as her breathing mocked my careless urgency. She sat up and pulled the shirt off over her head.

She wore nothing beneath. Her bare back shone before me and then she turned in a quick, self-conscious movement, showing herself to me. The narrow length of her neck, framed by her hair. The fall of her shoulders, marble smooth. The rounded, lifting nipple-budded breasts above her incurving belly. The pale flush of her skin.

The breathcalming pure pleasure of her made redundant any photograph. I felt no wish to rush ahead. Only I had to reach up and touch with privileged fingers the hard bud of each breast. A confirmation of reality; no self-abusive fantasy this. Then feast my eyes a while.

'I was with a bloke yesterday,' I said, needing to clear my throat before I could speak with confidence, 'who said that we are all users, that everybody uses everybody else. I suppose he meant there's no such thing as altruism.' I ran my hands over her breasts, down her bending sides: a tactile fragrance of flesh. 'Do you believe that?'

'I haven't thought about it.'

'And don't want to?'

Her eyes were closed. She shook her head. Waving hair. All of her body focused.

'Don't talk any more, word child,' she said.

She shifted her position, sitting so that *Don't talk, she says, but the mind* she could undo the buttons of my *goes on. Why won't it stop? Give up.*

Patterns of Lovemaking
There is not much point in trying to describe lovemaking—

shirt, which she accomplished slowly,
Give up itself to what is happening?
laying the shirt from my chest. Her
It damn well thinks, damn well goes on
cool, tender hands then moving over me,
thinking, watching what is happening
soothingly inflammatory, a beginning
like a spoiled indulged child. Shut
of physical crescendo.
up, damn you, shut it.
    Her hands ran down my chest,
There is dazzle-blue sky above
across my stomach. Found the clasp of my
framed in the tent door opening flap
jeans. Undid it. Drew down the zip.
door peak. Shut it. Say the nine times
Pushed jeans and pants below my knees.
table   once nine is nine two nines
    Cooling air feathered my loins.
are eighteen three nines are twenty-
A delicious greeting to my nakedness.
seven four nines are something or other
And Helen's hands, coming with the
five nines are more than that
breeze, hardly heavier of touch.
ten nines are ninety is easy
Searching, fondling, encouraging.
you just put the nought on   o god
    For moments that were
the pleasure   shut it   shut head
endlessly short this was all
close down   off the air   off in
I wished for, all I had ever

whether it is hand-
holding, embracing,
fondling or intercourse.
It is experienced as
a matter of emotion
and relationship
more than action.

    Though we think
of lovemaking as
instinctive, as indeed
it is primarily,
the patterns of expression
vary widely in different
parts of the world.
This shows that we
learn many aspects
of it while growing up—
from books,
movies and TV,
from what we notice
in parks and on beaches,
from what we see our
parents doing and
not doing. . . .

    In the more
drawnout love-
making, lips, tongue,
hands may make
loving contact with
lips, tongue, breasts or
genitals—for several
minutes or for many.
Each couple after

the air   ha   o god don't laugh
wanted.
laugh   please don't laugh   it's
  But then rising in me, a
not done   not done   not in the oven
gathering of every lusting sensation
yet   ha   o please don't laugh
flowing from every cell of my body
under my spread arm spread hands I feel
to that straining centre, wanted
grass knife-blade-sharp, coarse
body on body, a clutch of source
soil beneath grasp the crystal
of pleasure to whole possession.
earth no grasp her grasp shut it
  I grasped at her. For a fearful
enjoy enjoy enjoy enjoy enjoy enjoy
moment she was gone. But then
shut it words are like boulders
was back again.
thoughts are like broadsides fired
And naked.
against my bodypleasure   why?
As I was
o why?   o sylvan wyeswale
And as eager
is this what makes body
As blind
is this the howdyado   the I'm all
As grasping
right jack   the deflowering of ditto
As clinging
the cider rosie had

months and years
of variation tends
to settle on patterns
which give the
greatest mutual
pleasure. A few
couples even progress
all the way to the
climax of orgasm
while engaged in
the forms of lovemaking
which most people
consider only preliminary-
because in this manner
they reach ecstasy
more surely or
more pleasurably
than by genital
intercourse. For most
couples, however, the
ultimate desire is
for intercourse, in
which the man
inserts his erect
penis into the
woman's vagina. Her
labia and vagina have
been made more moist
than usual by her
excitement, so
the penis can slip in
more easily. The man
has the instinct to

124

As sinuous of body
is this the stars in
As flooded with strength
my eyes   my eyes   close my eyes
And energy
in excelsis
And fire.
shut it
She pulled at me,
is this the way
turning me over upon her, urgently,
aboard the lugger
as she fell back upon
and now let
the ground.
battle commence
And gave me entrance
just shut it
with a deep delighting sigh.
shut it
And then there were
shut it
no more
shut
words
it
no more
it
thoughts
It

Nothing but movement

thrust his hips
rhythmically back-
wards and forwards
to move the penis
partly out and in
again, to increase
the sensation for
both. Intercourse
can last fifteen seconds;
or a man can learn
to hold back his
orgasm so that
intercourse lasts
for fifteen minutes or
more. As the couple
come nearer to orgasm,
both partners usually
want the rhythmic motion to
become more vigorous
and the woman
may participate in it too.
At the moment of
orgasm—and
generous, experienced
lovers try to make their
climaxes come simultan-
eously—they are
overwhelmed by
five or ten seconds of
intense, pulsating
pleasure
while the ejaculation
occurs, and they cling

Body on

Flesh on flesh on

Mouth and hands and legs and
  thrusting
  driving
  wild
  relief
  felt
  during her
  high
  long
  scream

tightly together. After
orgasm there is
usually a feeling
of complete
satisfaction
and peace
which often
leads to sleep.
—*A Young Person's*
  Guide to
  Life and Love,
  by Dr Benjamin Spock,
  Bodley Head,
  1971.

Thought returns
A sense of place
Of being
exhausted flat-out quenched desireless body able still to pleasure
in the aftertaste of body on body made poignant by a reasonless
sense of loss sweet with gratitude but still no words to speak no
wish to say

126

Thanks.

You are kind, warm, funny and clever. And pretty good for a beginner. I wish I could be around to help you practice. But I'm not, and won't be. We wouldn't survive. Truly! We'd get all serious.

I'm afraid of that – not ready for it yet – if ever! But you've been a <u>help</u>. I hope I was to you. I doubt if we'll meet again. Not like today. But I will remember always.

Be loved.

H. xxx

END GAME

After Helen

When I woke, the sun was setting. Egg yolk in deepening blue.
My sleeping bag covered me. Helen's doing, I supposed.

I looked for her. Found not her, but her note lying by my
side weighted by a dalestone.

I read it.

Then lay back. Wordless thought.

Then, impulse:

I had to go back home. Whatever I had come for, I now had.
But had yet to sort out.

I felt good as soon as I moved, being busy again with purpose.
Whatever I am to be, I am not to be a drifter, a taker-or-leaver
of life. I know that now, if no more.

I ate the remains of our lunch, being hungry: stale bread,
evening dew moist; a mouthful of herring, acid in my dry sleep
mouth; a morsel of cheese; all washed down with water, plastic
coated from my aging bottle. Then sat again, feeling calmed,
reflective; gazed at the view as though wishing to cherish it, the
day, that time-and-place.

Till darkness fell. Ten thirty or thereabouts.

I was ready for off. I would have to walk. No buses now, no
money for private hire. Fifteen miles. But I wanted to walk.

Penance, payment or pleasure? Who cares?

I was going somewhere. Home.

The only one I have. For now.

I laughed.

An owl hooted. A barn owl. He was sitting on Willance's cold
grave stone. As I watched, he took off and ghosted into the
valley.

Tramping

Down into Richmond, silent dark town, through Skeeby. On up to Scotch Corner, across the slice of motorway and along the back road to Barton. Then Stapleton and the roundabout, junction of old road and motorway spur into Darlington. Across the bridge humping Yorkshire into County Durham. Then by Blackwell down to South Park, along Geneva Road's dull, stale mile. And home.

Roadwork at night is a kind of torture by monotony. Thoughts adopt a steady repetitive stomp to match your mechanical feet.

My thoughts that night tramped through Jacky and Robby and Helen and me.

Pedestrian stuff; all here, preceding.

Home

Hello, love.

Hi, Ma. Didn't mean to wake you.

I wasn't asleep. How've you got back?

Walked.

Walked? Where from?

Richmond.

At this time of night! It's nearly four.

I'd finished what I had to do so I came straight home.

I'm glad. But you must be worn out.

A bit.

And hungry. I'll cook you something.

No, no, Ma. Just a cup of tea, eh?

Are you sure? You ought to have something.

I'm okay, really.

Well, a cup of tea, eh?

How's Dad?

Much better.

Good.

Not right yet, you know. Never will be, I suppose. But he's sitting up and taking notice again.

That's good.

Thought I'd lost him.

O, I've a letter he gave me for you.

A letter?

Wrote it yesterday. Said if you rang I was to get an address where you could collect it. If you weren't coming back soon, like.

He's never written me a letter before.

He's hardly had need to, has he? You've not been away long before, not on your own.

But he didn't need to now, did he?

What's in it?

I don't know, love. You'd better read it and find out.

I'll take my tea and drink it upstairs, Ma. Okay?
All right, love. And get some sleep. You'll be worn out tomorrow.

The Memorial Hospital
Monday

My Dear Son,

I must be on the mend because they have let me set up and write this.

I am not much of a letter writer as you know, and not much of a talker neither. But being near death, as I have been, makes you think. I have been thinking about you and me, and your dear Mother of course. I have been thinking about the rows we have been having lately. Maybe it is just growing pains you are growing up and I am growing old. I want you to know that your Mother and me are very proud of you and have always tried to do our best for you to the utmost of our ability.

the school has brought you on well, especially Mr. Midgely, and your mother and me are very grateful. But sometimes I get worried because I cannot always understand what you are doing.

I am not trying to make excuses though. Maybe we should both try harder to see each other's point of view. I know I will if I pull through this present bit of bother which I hope I do for your Mother's sake.

Now what I am really writing to you about is this. I want you to do something. I want you to look under the hankies in the top drawer of the bureau in our room. There is a little box there. I want you to have it and contents from me with my love and as a token of my sincere regard for you.

Your loving
Dad.

Free Gift

A small, black, firm-bodied box, no bigger than a wallet, edges worn, as though from much handling. Inside, red silk plush. Laid in the plush, two medals, pristine, with bright red, gold and blue striped ribbons. On the medals, raised in bas relief, the picture of a racing motorcyclist. On the reverse an inscription:

NATIONAL TRIALS CHAMPIONSHIP
JUNIOR CLASS
FIRST

NATIONAL TRIALS CHAMPIONSHIP
ALL COMERS CLASS
THIRD

Each also inscribed with Dad's name and a date.

He would have been eighteen.

Kitchentalk

You're still up, Ma.
I'm not tired, love.
He's given me these.
Yes? Very nice.
Why?
He wanted to, I expect.
They mean a lot to him?
They do.
He's never mentioned them. I've never seen them before.
It's just the way he is.
You know about them?
Yes.
Can you tell me?

When he was young, he wanted to be a motorcycle racer. He went to the Isle of Man T.T. races every year to watch. 'Course, then it was bigger than it is now. I'm talking about thirty years ago. He got a bike of his own as soon as he could. Bullied his mother into buying him one on the H.P., I think. And he started trials racing on it.

Racing across country?
Yes. He did well. Won them medals the last time he did it. He was eighteen. He decided after that it was time for the real thing. But he needed a new bike for professional stuff. And he wanted to enter the T.T. Something like that.

And?
His father wouldn't hear of it. Put a stop to it.
Why?
Said it was too dangerous and cost too much.
But how could he stop Dad if he really wanted to do it?
Well, for a start your dad didn't have the money. Not for a new bike, fares, racing expenses, all that.
And his father wouldn't help?
No.

Wasn't Dad earning enough?

As an apprentice joiner? That's what he was then.

So he never did it?

No. His father said he could do what he liked when he was out of his apprenticeship at twenty-one but that till then he'd do as he was told. And in those days you had to pay more heed to your parents than people do now.

But didn't he try when he was twenty-one?

Too late then. He meant to. But he'd never have caught the competition by then. And anyhow, how could he do it all on a joiner's pay? No, he had an old bike and roared round the streets like a madman and went to the T.T. as a spectator. But he never raced again.

Does he regret it?

Why don't you ask him?

Silly question.

Perhaps. But I'd still ask him.

Thanks, Ma.

Get some sleep now, love. Goodnight.

Making Room

I sat a while in my room. Needing to. Not disturbed, but wanting quiet. Peace. Stillness.

But soon the walls were falling on me.

Unhurried, a deliberate act conducted with great care, I began to disrobe the walls of their covering of posters and pictures. Took them all down; piled them one on another in an old suitcase.

Did not stop at the pictures. The ornaments, bric-à-brac, oddments of all sorts. All the left-overs of me. All into the suitcase.

With surprise I found myself adding some of the books. Not all. Those which impulse told me were sloughed-off skins.

Me, past. Other people's me.

Last of all, I placed Helen's letter, her photograph, and Morgan's *Charges Against Literature* into a large envelope. Sealed it. Placed it on top of all else.

Shut the suitcase. Locked it. Stowed it neatly, at the back of a cupboard in the spare bedroom, among all the rest of the family's lumber.

Put the key into my father's medal case beside his—my—pristine medals.

Now my room was nude, but for some books, and, alone on my desk, the medals in their worn case.

Coffeetalk

'An odd concoction,' said Morgan, coffee expectorating from his plastic mug on to the sixth-form commonroom floor as he and Ditto made for two empty seats in a corner.

'We have discussed the inadequacy of the coffee before,' said Ditto.

'I mean your masterwork,' Morgan said.

They sat, pulling their chairs together, side by side, facing a window providing a view of the breaktime mayhem in the playground below.

'Did you find it distasteful?' asked Ditto.

'Not that. But there are some points I want to argue with you.'

'What then?'

'Amusing sometimes, embarrassing sometimes, interesting sometimes.'

'How generous of you.'

'You had quite a time during half term.'

'I did,' said Ditto noncommittally.

'But to be honest . . .'

'Why not?'

'. . . I can't agree that this curious document answers my Charges.'

'You disappoint me, Morgan.'

'Then demonstrate.'

'What a laboratory mind you do have.'

Morgan smiled with self-satisfaction.

'All right,' said Ditto. 'Point by point but briefly. Point one: is it a story?'

'Of a kind,' Morgan conceded with reluctance. 'The events of your week past.' He chortled at his pun.

Ditto allowed the ambiguity to pass apparently unnoticed. Two could play at double takes, and at sleight of mind.

'Point two: you are only concerned with truth. Have you had truth?'

137

'Allowing for the inadequacy of your skills as a reporter, yes.'

'My modest work convinced you in this respect?'

'Sufficiently for our purpose.'

'Good. Point three: would you agree that my account does not pretend that life is neat, tidy, falsely logical—any of those things to which you objected, you'll remember?'

'Granted. It's a right rag-bag!' Morgan laughed loudly.

'I'm pleased I amuse you.'

'You do, you do.'

'Point four: literature is only a game, an amusing pretence, a lie I think you said. Playing at life, wasn't it?'

'Correct.'

'Is my poor effort?'

Morgan sat up, as though springing a trap. 'I thought that was where you were headed. False logic.'

'Why?'

'Because, matey, I was talking about fiction. Remember! And your little masterwork isn't fiction.'

'O?' said Ditto.

The klaxon sounded the end of morning break.

'Of course it isn't,' bayed Morgan, triumphant. 'We've already agreed about that. It is a record of what happened to you last week.'

'That's what *you* said. I only asked if it convinced you in that respect. You said yes.'

'Are you playing games?'

'Do you mean, have I written fiction?'

'Declare!'

'Could be. How do you know I didn't sit in my room at home all week making the stuff up?'

'I don't believe you.'

'Thank you. That's the best compliment you could pay me.'

'But your father is ill, you're not lying about that, are you?'

'Of course not . . .'

'Well then . . .'

'All fiction starts from something.'

138

'Look, I've got Taylor now. He brooks no lateness. We'll settle this over lunch.'

'A viva I shall enjoy.'

Morgan made for the door.

'I'm in the thing,' he said as he went. 'Are you saying I'm just a character in a story?'

'Aren't we all?' said Ditto and laughed.